Martin Millar was born in Scotland and now lives in

*rewolf
f New*
as the
r noir'.

AIF

KT-470-637

OCT 2016

Visit Martin Millar at:
www.martinmillar.com
Twitter: MartinMillar1

Praise for Martin Millar:

'Undeniably brilliant' *Guardian*

'The funniest writer in Britain today' *GQ*

'Martin Millar writes like Kurt Vonnegut
might have written, if he'd been born fifty years later
in a different country and hung around with entirely
the wrong sort of people' Neil Gaiman

'Imagine Kurt Vonnegut reading Marvel Comics
with The Clash thrashing in the background.
For the deceptively simple poetry of the
everyday, nobody does it better' *List*

'The master of urban angst' *i-D Magazine*

Supercute Futures

MARTIN MILLAR

piatkus

PIATKUS

First published in Great Britain in 2018 by Piatkus

1 3 5 7 9 10 8 6 4 2

A CIP catalogue record for this book
is available from the British Library.

ISBN 978-0-349-41934-3

Typeset in Sabon by M Rules
Printed and bound by CPI Group (UK) Ltd, Croydon, CR0 4YY

Papers used by Piatkus are from well-managed forests
and other responsible sources.

MIX
Paper from
responsible sources
FSC® C104740

Piatkus
An imprint of
Little, Brown Book Group
Carmelite House
50 Victoria Embankment
London EC4Y 0DZ

An Hachette UK Company
www.hachette.co.uk

www.littlebrown.co.uk

Mitsu liked her therapist. He was comforting. He assured her it wasn't her fault that Budapest had been so badly damaged.

'As I understand it, C19 had no choice but to let it happen.'

'Not really. Not after what happened to Volgograd. Can't do that to a Russian city and not suffer any consequences.'

It had taken a long time to find a therapist she really liked. She'd tried many different models. Mox had to like him too because they were always sharing therapists. They'd tried having one each but it had never worked out. Each of them would be too curious about the other's so they'd end up going to both. Really, they preferred sharing. They'd been like that since they were three years old, when they'd first met at the advanced nursery school.

'I just wish I hadn't been involved. There were a lot of casualties.'

'It could have been much worse if C19 had allowed retaliation.'

Their therapist was so well-spoken. They'd adjusted his accent, pushed it back to a type of cultured English rarely heard these days. Almost as cultured as Mox, and she'd modelled her accent on the previous Queen.

'You might say your actions saved lives. No reprisals brought hostilities to an end.'

Mitsu looked down at her legs. Soft pink slippers, bright pink stockings ending four centimetres below her small silver shorts. Her hair swung in front of her eyes. It was silver, yellow, purple, pink and blue. Here in Supercute

1

space it was controlled by Big Colour Super V-Hair; outside it was biologically enhanced. In either it could be any length, any thickness, any combination of colours.

'You could say it saved lives. But when we started Supercute, we never thought we'd end up discussing which military action might or might not be supported.'

'I'd say you've both coped very well with all the changes you've seen.'

He was so reassuring. Grey-haired, well-dressed, well-spoken. Mitsu liked her therapist. He always made her feel better. She remembered back to the time when artificial intelligence hadn't advanced far enough for truly effective psychology. Both she and Mox had been obliged to visit human therapists. They'd never been as good.

The show would be starting soon. She touched a button on her wrist and the therapy room faded away.

Morioka Sachi, director, brought on Presenter Bear. It was almost time for the *Supercute Show*, flagship of the gigantic global corporation that was Supercute Enterprises, founded a long time ago by two young teenage girls in a bedroom in London, with only an iPhone and a collection of their favourite cuddly toys.

In their dressing room, Mox and Mitsu reclined patiently in their make-up chairs as four tiny drones hovered in front of them, applying the finishing touches to their cosmetics and the final tweaks to their hair. They'd designed the colouring program themselves, writing their own code when the best commercial programs didn't give them quite the extravagantly cute results they were looking for, and their multi-coloured hair was now imitated by their millions of youthful fans around the world.

2

Two of the tiny drones withdrew, allowing others to take their places, these drones being responsible for attaching the tiny hearts and stars to Mox and Mitsu's faces so that a colourful array of pink, blue and red shapes ran down their cheeks. Next came the sticking plaster over their noses, pink with a picture of Small Cute Presenter, a stylised kitten which was a fan favourite and a big seller.

Sachi's voice sounded in the dressing room. 'Three minutes, ladies.'

On stage, Presenter Bear strode out to welcome the audience, those watching around the world and those here in Supercute space. Presenter Bear was another popular character, an endearing fluffy brown bear whose image could currently be seen projecting from cereal packets all around the world.

'Is everyone ready for the Supercute girls?'

The audience screamed that *yes, they were*.

Mox and Mitsu stood up. Mitsu looked down at her feet. She was wearing a delicate pair of embroidered slippers. She spoke one word.

'Platform.'

Her slippers transformed, the thin soles extending by twelve centimetres, the uppers stretching up over her ankles, till she wore the platforms favoured by Supercute. They were striking, distinctive, and rather impractical, unless, like Mox and Mitsu, you'd had a lot of practice. Mox did the same, transforming her shoes. 'Reflections,' said Mitsu. A holographic duplicate of each girl popped into existence in front of them, rotating slowly. They studied their appearances, checking for any minute detail that might be wrong. Supercute never let down their audience. Mox examined the hem of her lavender skirt, beneath which showed four centimetres of her thighs,

3

in accordance with the Supercute Style Manual, the rest of her legs being covered by matching lavender stockings.

'You look fantastic, Mitsu.'

'So do you!'

They smiled at each other. Like their friendship, their love of cute and colourful clothes had never worn thin. They heard the sound of their theme tune, 'Destination Supercute'. It was loud, raucous, more so than might have been expected from their appearance. But they were idiosyncratic in that way and always had been. The *Supercute Show* had not developed from the judgements, opinions and marketing requirements of a corporate board; it had developed from the two girls' individual tastes and their brilliance at relating to their audience.

A new screen opened in front of them. Ms Gibbs, production assistant, smiled at them. 'It's time.'

'We're on our way.'

They left the dressing room. Outside, two uniformed security guards escorted them towards the set. Mox and Mitsu strode along purposefully but when they neared the stage, their gait changed, so as they appeared in front of their audience there was a hint of fragility about them, a slight impression of delicacy which made you think they might need protection from the harsh world outside. In reality they were both so comprehensively enhanced with the most advanced biotech available, they'd have been unlikely to come to harm if a truck crashed into them, but that wasn't the image they wanted to project. Their voices changed subtly too, so that they both sounded younger. Mox and Mitsu spoke sixteen languages and they could produce this effect in all of them.

*

4

Presenter Bear ambled around the stage. He appeared solid and moved realistically, just the way he would have if he were real, if there could have been such a thing as a real, human-sized anthropomorphised brown bear with large brown eyes and a winning smile.

'We're the world's number one show, from London to Rio, from Paris to Tokyo! Here they are, Mox and Mitsu, the Supercute girls!'

Mox and Mitsu walked onto a stage that was colourful, cheerful, chaotic, noisy, and above everything else, cute. Colours were bright but never garish, the spectrum selected with infinite care so that nothing clashed. Everywhere you looked there were characters not met in the real world: tiny *chibi* figures scampering about, laughing and playing; smiling cupcakes and friendly strawberries sliding down miniature rainbows into comforting bento boxes. Sleepy kittens lay on plump pink cushions. Stars floated overhead, pink and blue like those on Mox and Mitsu's faces.

A stream of fans from all around the world appeared momentarily on stage, laughing and waving to the audience before fading out of the space which merged with the real-life performers. Supercute elements were everywhere, in clothing and stage design. Bears were a prevailing theme but there were other animals too, kittens and rabbits and pandas and robins, and the plump dinosaur, *Blue Bronto*, a firm favourite, which had sold more copies around the world than any other soft toy.

The music increased in volume and for thirty seconds or so the musicians were visible, all dressed in tartan and black, a stylized version of a school band. Talented musicians, they'd become famous through their association with Supercute. They made a thunderous noise, again not quite the sound that might have been expected from the surroundings. The *Supercute Show* had always featured rock music and pop music from Europe and Japan, never once playing anything American.

Mox smiled broadly and waved. 'Hello Europe! Hello what's left of Asia and America!'

Mitsu waved too. 'Hello Australia, hello Africa!'

In the control room, Morioka Sachi deftly manipulated the transparent screens in front of her before selecting some suitable-looking fans to bring on stage.

Six Nigerians, aged twelve or thirteen, appeared beside Mox and Mitsu, all dressed in their Supercute fan clothes, a great wave of bright pastels, short skirts, colourful T-shirts with slogans, tiny lavender cardigans layered over pink blouses, platform shoes, some wearing the popular Supercute medical masks in pink, light blue and white. Everyone entering Supercute space seemed to have extraordinary long, thick, brightly coloured hair in multiple shades. Most used the *Supercute Big Colour Super V-Hair* package that was an essential item for all Supercute fans. While they might not be able to have, in real life, extraordinary hair like Mox and Mitsu, they could in all the Fun Worlds created by Supercute.

Some of the cute and colourful clothes were real, worn at home and translated into Supercute space. Others existed only in that space. Many of them had been bought from MitsuMox Global Merchandise, but there were other outfits which were either homemade or adapted from older items. Mox and Mitsu never insisted on their fans wearing Supercute brands. In fact, they encouraged people to make their own. (Despite this, their own brands sold in huge numbers around the world.)

The fans danced and waved to everyone before Sachi faded them out again. Mox and Mitsu walked through the mass of cheerful characters, laughing as tiny *chibis* bounced around on their shoulders before jumping back to their companions. A miniature pink tornado tousled their hair then vanished. As they approached the front of the stage, the main camera angle focused very briefly, as if accidentally, on their slender bodies, before moving upwards to their beautiful, smiling faces. The show was aimed at preteens and teens, and presented as suitable for all ages, but for some teens, and older viewers, Mox and Mitsu provided an additional element of sex. They were well aware of this. It was never stressed but nor was it ever absent.

Mox waved. 'Always nice to see our friends from Nigeria. Keep hanging in there! What have we got on the show tonight, Mitsu?'

'All our favourites! There's a new episode of *Supercute Space Warriors* and we'll be talking to Shanina right afterwards.'

Shanina Space Warrior was a tremendously popular character. She led her crew through all kinds of adventures in the galaxy, displaying intelligence, bravery and a liking for Supercute outfits second only to Mox and Mitsu themselves. Despite being a fictional character she was often interviewed on the show. Many viewers had long ago forgotten that she wasn't actually real.

'Then we have the *Supercute Fashion Show*, a roundup of every new design in the new SuperGlam SuperNails pack, a report from the Supercute relief mission in Jayapura – our valocopter pilots have been busy – then we'll be giving some tips for how to get through level six of *Supercute Space Warriors nine*, still top of the gaming charts after thirty-six weeks. We've got some fabulous new wings for Supercute Fairy Realm, and after that—'

As if from nowhere, a small shower of water sprayed through the air, touching the girls. They laughed as if it were a cheerful surprise.

'What's that?' Mox looked round.

'It's De-Sal Dim Dim!' cried Mitsu.

There was cheering from the audience as De-Sal Dim Dim bounced into view. De-Sal Dim Dim, the very cute logo of Supercute Greenfield, was another popular character. He appeared on stage as a smiling green figure about one metre tall. His face was already familiar in most countries in the world, visual representative of the huge desalinisation and environmental restoration business owned by Supercute. Since the multitude of natural disasters that had made the purification of sea water vitally important in every region, Supercute Greenfield had become one of the world's largest companies. Their desalinisation plants could be seen on coastlines everywhere.

De-Sal Dim Dim spread his arms and sang.

> 'De-Sal Dim Dim cleans your water
> Make it safe for your son and daughter!
> Nice clean water from the sea
> Yummy goodness for you and me!'

De-Sal sprayed more computer-generated water around and the crowd on stage shrieked and laughed. Mitsu leaned over to talk to him. 'How's life in the world of desalinisation, De-Sal?'

'Wonderful! I've purified so much water in Portugal they've managed to grow some trees!'

Trees appeared on stage, to fantastic applause. Mox seemed very impressed. 'That's great news, De-Sal!'

De-Sal Dim Dim burst into song again.

> *'There's a little problem in Mexico*
> *They've got no water and the plants won't grow*
> *But I'm going there to help them out*
> *Oh Mexico, I'll end your drought!'*

Ms Mason, Chief Executive Officer of RX Enviro, sat in her boardroom with senior vice presidents Mr Hernandez and Mr Schulze, watching the *Supercute Show*. Mr Hernandez grunted in annoyance. 'These Supercute bitches are not getting their hands on Mexico's water rights.'

Ms Mason showed no emotion as she replied, though it was a serious matter. 'They already have. Once ZanZan signs the contract for attack drones, the deal's done.'

A large representation of the ongoing *Supercute Show* floated in front of them. Ms Mason watched dispassionately; Mr Hernandez with interest, as he knew his children loved Mox and Mitsu; Mr Schulze showed irritation. If Ms Mason insisted on holding board meetings in RX Enviro space, he wished she wouldn't fill it with nature. Business, in his opinion, should not be done with the stars above and a waterfall behind. Adding to his ire, he loathed Supercute.

'The Central American Recovery Body should never have allowed Supercute ZanZan to expand into their territory.'

'They couldn't stop them,' said Ms Mason. 'Supercute would have rolled the appropriation committee over. They own all these people.'

'Supercute and ZanZan Defence. A match made in hell. Why did C19 let them get together?'

'C19 remains neutral as long as no one rocks the boat too much.'

Mr Hernandez shook his head. 'If no one rocks the boat in our favour, RX Enviro is heading down the indexes and straight into history.'

RX Enviro were a huge operator in the fields of desalinisation and environmental repair. For the past five years they'd been losing out to Supercute Greenfield and the situation was becoming critical.

'If we lose all the Mexican desalinisation contracts to Supercute we're finished.'

Above them the stars shone in a brilliant array. Mr Schulze frowned. When he'd first joined the company, you attended meetings by walking into a room and sitting at the table. He didn't see that these gatherings in RX Enviro space were any great improvement. A discreet buzzer sounded, from an unseen secretary.

'Ms Mason, it's almost time for your call with Moe Bennie at Lark 3 Media.'

A small transparent screen appeared in front of Ms Mason. She touched it. Moe Bennie's data file appeared, his profile rotating on screen and financial figures running below. Moe Bennie was, from his appearance at least, a nineteen-year-old youth with a taste in clothes not dissimilar to Supercute. He had long, light blue hair, rather large blue eyes, and wore a long pink coat over a dark blue shirt, or possibly blouse.

Mr Shultz shuddered. 'Not another of these cutesy freaks.' He had few points of reference to make sense of Moe Bennie's appearance. Mr Hernandez did because he'd seen people like Moe Bennie in his children's games. He looked like one of those characters his daughter liked who fought aliens with his magic space sword. Something like that anyway. Mr Hernandez hadn't paid that close attention.

'He has an interesting proposition,' said Ms Mason, calmly.

Mox and Mitsu took a break after their dance segment, letting Plumpy Panda lead viewers through the piece on Supercute's current relief mission. Supercute space was suddenly full of pink and white valocopters taking supplies to the trapped and starving population of Jayapura. Anyone connected to Supercute space was able to get on board and watch as aid was delivered by the Supercute female pilots, themselves celebrities, all dressed in the well-known Supercute camouflage. This was four shades of pink and had been fashioned by Mox and Mitsu themselves, basing it on a Danish army design which had long since disappeared from the world.

Mox and Mitsu sat backstage, sipping green tea, resting after their dance. They'd put a lot of effort into it as they always did, enough to tire even their enhanced bodies. These days they were brilliant dancers though neither of them had been especially gifted when young. They'd always been enthusiastic and confident enough to spend time on dance floors in London nightclubs when they were teenagers, but it hadn't featured on their show in the beginning. They'd added dancing skills to their repertoire later, studying the art quite meticulously, the same way they'd studied mathematics and languages at school, physics and computer sciences at university. When they began to earn money from their show they'd hired instructors, learned their favourite moves from J-pop and K-pop, widened their knowledge with visits to modern dance recitals and the English National Ballet, ending up as extremely talented performers. These days they'd added dance programs to their internal knowledge banks. With their own skills, software assistance, and their enhanced bodies, their dancing was now quite spectacular, admired even by people who didn't care for their show.

While they rested, the latest episode of *Supercute Space Warriors* played. Around the world, Supercute fans adjusted their visors to join in with the adventures of Shanina Space Warrior and her crew, travelling with them from planet to planet and galaxy to galaxy, battling foes, discovering lost empires, and coping with the on-board romances which occurred surprisingly frequently. For the past two months, Marizana, the rather shy young navigator, had found herself courted by no less than three of the Space Warriors, and the romantic entanglements generated by this had sent a large proportion of Supercute fandom into a frenzy. *Supercute Space Warriors* was a huge franchise, the show and the game both generating a vast turnover in physical and downloadable merchandise of all sorts. Shanina Space Warrior could be found on hundreds of products, her picture second in popularity only to those of Mox and Mitsu themselves.

Mitsu tripped daintily across the stage. 'Time for the *Supercute Fashion Show*!'

Mox teetered after her. 'Supercute fashion from around the world!'

From their homes all over the still-habitable parts of the globe, more fans now entered Supercute space where they danced and paraded around, showing off their colourful outfits and toys, many carrying their favourite Supercute fluffy animal, *chibi* or company logo. One group would fade out and another would appear, brought there by Sachi and her assistants whose array of screens, cameras and sensors identified people who'd look good on stage. Mox and Mitsu announced some of their visitors as they appeared.

'Here's Nurul and Aisha from Malaysia!'

'Gabi from Germany!'

'Hendrik from Mokusei Moon Village 3. He's connected via Supercute satellite!'

'Six girls from the UN Togo Protectorate!'

Attaching bright plastic clips over the already colourful layers below, all the fans from the Protectorate had taken particular care with their Big Colour Super V-hair. (Mox had flatly refused a request from marketing to spell *colour* as *color*, telling them that while civilisation might be having a difficult time, it had not yet ended.)

'Here's Reem and Marwa from the Permanent Refugee Settlement at Misrata!' Mitsu beamed at them. 'Nice Supercute radiation masks, girls!'

As Mitsu spoke, her outfit changed, her blouse shifting from Supercute Lavender Three to Supercute Lavender Nine, an automatic adjustment to compensate for a change in the stage lighting. Reem and Marwa from the Permanent Refugee Settlement waved happily to everyone, and though you couldn't make out much of their faces behind their radiation masks, it was obvious they were smiling.

Mox talked to the same therapist as Mitsu.

'We lifted the whole Supercute thing from Japan. We loved anything that was *kawaii*. We were just kids in a bedroom in London doing a web show with an iPhone.

13

Weren't doing any harm. We never could have predicted it would end up like this.'

'Like what?'

'With us being one of the nineteen conglomerates who effectively rule a large part of the world.'

'Your background must be very different from most of C19.'

Mox nodded. 'It is. Not many of the people running these organisations started off with nothing. We did. We had no money, no backing, nothing. We started a tiny show on YouTube and built it up into a global entertainment network, just by being good at it.' She paused, thinking back. 'But after that, we were fortunate. Desalinisation. We'd invested in a small company who came up with a much better way to purify seawater just when most of the world's fresh water supply dried up. Every continent was crying out for water and we could get it to them quicker and cheaper than anyone else. We could hardly build plants fast enough. Huge permanent installations, and emergency supplies for drought relief. In a couple of years we owned this gigantic environmental construction business which just swallowed up the competition. Not what we envisaged when we started playing with cute skirts and cuddly toys.'

Mox paused again. The therapist let her sit in silence for a few moments. The room was still and peaceful, with no moving pictures or holograms. 'We made a lot of friends in Tokyo back then – all the kids with cute clothes in Harajuku, Shibuya, Aoyama. We were copying their style, which was fine when we were small. I don't know what they'd have made of us becoming so successful with it. None of them lived to see it, anyway. Harajuku disappeared in tsunami number five and most of the rest of Tokyo in the next one. When they built New Tokyo, it was never really the same.'

A discreet doorbell sounded, followed by Mitsu's voice.

'Can I come in?'

Mox smiled. 'Sure.'

Mitsu materialised in the room. She sat next to Mox on the couch, close so their arms touched.

'You sneaked off to therapy quickly.'

Mox screwed up her face. 'I felt a little bad seeing our fans in radiation masks.'

'They might not be our fault. ZanZan aren't the only ones selling battlefield nuclear weapons. We have to go, we need to talk to the combined board before the transfer.'

'I thought we had some time?'

'We're scheduled to get our shoulder replacements first.'

Mox looked at her shoulder. 'This one's lasted a long time, it'll do for a while.'

Mitsu smiled. 'Come on, it won't take long. This skeleton upgrade will see us into another century.'

Mitsu's English was perfect, as was Mox's Japanese. They'd taught each other their native languages a long time ago.

'I wish we could just slot these new bits in without surgery. Like we used to slot new memory into a computer. Remember when you still had to do that?'

'Of course. First time we did it was at the advanced nursery school, when we were four. We knew how to do it before that, but they wouldn't let us dismantle laptops when we were three.'

Mox touched an invisible button on her wrist. The therapist and therapy room faded away, leaving Mox and Mitsu sitting in one of their offices. Mox glanced at one of the mirrors that floated in the corner.

'Do you think I should get a new face?'

'Don't be silly. The world loves your face. And mine. We were joint *Most Beautiful Celebrities* this year.'

'We own the show that gave us the award.'

'No we don't, it's independent. We own the one that gave us the *Cutest Noses* award.'

'Right. I was forgetting.'

'And we were *Cutest Eyes and Ears* the year before. So no messing with our faces!'

The land shown on the screen was parched, withered, heavily polluted. The voiceover was serious, almost sombre.

'... *when RX Enviro began working on the San Bernardino–Sacramento coastline, smog and particulates had reached 8.6 on the Chansin index, ground toxins were at 7.9, and 93% of the region's water supply was rated poor or worse by the Emergency Federal Health Authority.*'

The voiceover took on a more optimistic tone.

'*Just look at the difference RX Enviro are making!*

There were shots of clean rivers, vines, green fields, even clear skies.

'*RX Enviro – number one choice for pollution control and impact clean-up.*'

Meeting the board of RX Enviro in their space, Moe Bennie didn't look impressed. 'Nice commercial,' he said to Ms Mason. 'If only you had the means to carry on the good work.'

'We're still restructuring our financing.'

Moe Bennie smiled. Ms Mason, a woman who was partial to the most formal business attire, did nonetheless admire his long, light blue hair. It was such a good match for his eyes, which were large, bright and clear.

'RX Enviro are in difficulties, Ms Mason.'

'Which makes it all the stranger you're looking to borrow three hundred billion from us.'

'It will be a sound investment on your part.'

'To do what, exactly?'

'It's half of the six hundred billion it will take to bring Supercute down.'

Senior Vice President Hernandez was dismissive. 'There's no way you can do it for that. That's a fraction of their listing and they've probably got ten times that stashed away.'

'It won't matter,' said Moe Bennie. 'They won't be able to bring it into play.'

'Are you talking about some sort of corporate raid?' Mr Schulze was no more enthusiastic than Mr Hernandez. 'You know that hasn't worked for half a century. Be as well sending a pirate ship.'

'You're going to have to give us a lot more detail before we help you,' said Ms Mason.

'Time is running out for RX Enviro, Ms Mason. You're dead the moment Supercute signs the deal in Mexico. That's about twelve hours from now.'

'That doesn't mean we're going to throw three hundred billion in your direction.'

Above Ms Mason, a red dawn was breaking in the boardroom. Birds could be heard faintly in the distance.

'Just supposing you had a credible plan for bringing Supercute down, what would C19 say? They're not just going to ignore a major destabilisation like that.'

Moe Bennie hosted his own show and was used to appearing in front of an audience. He talked to the board of RX Enviro with the same easy confidence he used to charm his teenage fans. 'We're not the only ones alarmed by Supercute ZanZan. Supercute being the biggest media corporation in the world was OK. Supercute becoming one of the largest environmental players was surprising, but still OK. Supercute joining up with ZanZan Defence is not OK. In two years' time they'll be rivalling the biggest arms manufacturers on the planet. Goodrich ATK and Chang Norinco aren't thrilled about that.'

'Are you saying they're on board?'

'I'm saying that a hundred billion each will persuade them to turn a blind eye to any irregularities.' Moe Bennie leaned forward. 'You have to face reality, Ms Mason. If you do nothing, RX Enviro will be pushed out of the market by Supercute. You'll lose your place on C19. After that, I wouldn't give much for the chances of your company surviving in any form. The others will pick you to pieces. Either you help me fight Supercute or you go under.'

Mox and Mitsu linked arms as they walked along the corridor. They could often be seen arm in arm, or hand in hand, in public.

'Can you believe it's been sixty years since our first body mod?'

'I know! Our first new, improved hearts. Quite primitive by today's standards.'

Most unexpectedly, an alarm sounded, something that never happened in the security of their own headquarters. There was immediate mayhem in the corridor as the efficient Supercute security guards poured out to protect the girls. In seconds Mox and Mitsu were shielded by a circle of armed men. Outside the immediate protective circle stood several Supercute security holograms, human-sized cute teddy bears carrying shock batons, used by many security forces these days as the friendly face of crowd control. As the chaos cleared, the guards, led by Captain Edwards, could be seen pointing their weapons at a confused-looking young man with a script-writer's pad in his hand.

Mitsu peered out from behind a security guard. 'Ranbir? What the hell?'

Mox's head poked out too. 'You set off the ag-scan again!'

Ranbir hung his head. 'Sorry.'

Mox and Mitsu emerged from the huddle to confront him. The guards did not yet lower their weapons.

'You know you can't come on this floor thinking aggressive thoughts,' said Mitsu.

'I wasn't!'

'You were obviously thinking something bad about us or you wouldn't have set off the ag-scan. What is it?'

'I didn't like the cuts you made in the last sketch I wrote,' explained Ranbir, sheepishly.

'So you thought you'd storm up here and complain?'

'Something like that ...'

Mox stepped forward. 'For God's sake, Ranbir, next time send it through the proper channels. We've got ag-scans protecting us from all aggressive intentions and if you set them off again we'll let the bloody guards shoot you.' She turned to Captain Edwards, their security chief, and addressed him politely. 'Thank you, Captain. It's all right now.'

'Yes, Ms Bennet.'

Ranbir scurried off, back downstairs to the writers' room, watched all the way by the security guards, and tracked by the ag-scans which were placed all around the upper floors of the building, ensuring that no one could come near to Mox and Mitsu while thinking aggressive thoughts. When they were finally satisfied that there was no danger, the guards holstered their weapons and retired from the scene.

There was a lot of hidden weaponry in Supercute headquarters, something which would at one time have been illegal, but was now permitted to those who privately policed their own property. Supercute owned a huge tract of land in the northeast of the city, an area once known as Barking and Dagenham, which had been largely flooded and destroyed before being reclaimed for commercial use. It was fenced, guarded, and housed Mox and Mitsu's headquarters, from where they produced the show. Mostly they lived there too, though they had other properties in the city, and hubs all around the world.

Their headquarters had been purpose-built and they were comfortable there, remaining mainly in the collection of buildings which were securely walled and fenced off from the outside world. Not far south their support squadron was stationed in a barracks, ready for any emergency. Outside the walls and fences they'd left some of their land derelict as a sort of buffer zone. Were land prices ever to rise again, they might build on it, but prices had been depressed for years and there was no sign of an improvement. Every city in the country had derelict, deserted areas, and in London many of these areas were now worthless; flooded, sunken and irradiated.

They carried on towards their medical centre. Dr Prasad greeted them with a smile.

'Ready for your new shoulders?'

'I suppose so,' muttered Mox.'

'We're ready.' Mitsu smiled back. She'd always found their body modifications easier to accept than Mox. Not that Mox had ever turned any of the enhancements down. Doing so would have been foolish. Here they were, far older than their audience, yet still regarded as the cutest and prettiest twenty-one-year-olds in the world. Since the impacts, the wars and the plenitude of other disasters that had left much of the planet uninhabitable, and much of the remaining population in poverty, none of their millions of fans had ever shown the slightest resentment that Mox and Mitsu carried on year after year, brighter, more colourful, more energetic and more beautiful than ever. On the contrary, they expected it, and even depended on it.

Mitsu reclined in her chair as she talked to her therapist. On the floor to her left was a small arrangement of stones, an indoor fragment of a Zen garden. She'd designed it especially for their therapy room.

'I was born in Japan but I don't have any infant memories of it because my parents moved to England when I was one. I didn't go back again till I was twelve. So I grew up in a Japanese household, in England. It was dissociative in a way, but not really a problem because home was very stable. Dad was in charge of the electronics factory and mum did her paintings. Mox didn't have such a good time as a child. Not at first, anyway.'

'What happened?'

'Her mother died in childbirth, in the ambulance. When they reached the hospital the new baby Mox was alive and her mother was dead. Her dad never got over it. He committed suicide one year later. So she was fostered out when I first met her at the advanced nursery school. We were three years old. Soon after that she came to live with us. Since then, we've never been apart.'

Mitsu ended her therapy and came back to reality in the operating theatre. Mox lay beside her. They remained fully conscious as their shoulder joints were replaced, feeling nothing after the appropriate nerves were switched off by their surgeons. Doctors stood over them while small white medical drones hovered overhead. Everyone in the room wore a Supercute medical mask, white, trimmed with pink and light blue. Those worn by the doctors were practical; those on Mox and Mitsu, more stylish. They lay close together, talking to each other, apparently unaffected by the procedure. Mox glanced down at her open shoulder. Inside there was no longer anything that looked human, her entire frame having been gradually replaced by light metals, carbon, silicone, and artificial biological material.

'It's still weird seeing all this machinery inside us.'

'At least blood doesn't pour out any more.' Mitsu smiled. 'Remember my eighth birthday when I fell off that swing?

Mox smiled too at the memory. 'I thought the bleeding would never stop. You really messed up that ambulance.'

'Our first year at Oxford.'

'You couldn't go to lectures for a week and I stayed with you in the hospital.'

'I always appreciated that. You've never liked hospitals.'

There was a discreet whirring sound as the doctors put the new shoulder joints in place, the final intricate nerve connections being made by the drones, some of which were tiny enough to do their work inside the artificial bone structure.

Mox frowned. 'What were we doing playing on swings?'

'I don't know. I guess we were still kids, in a way.' Mitsu paused. 'I don't think we ever went to the park again.'

Dr Prasad, as the presiding surgeon, kept careful watch as new enhanced skin was laid over the improved shoulders. 'Almost finished. The procedure has been successful.'

'Of course,' said Mitsu, from her prone position. 'We trust you completely, Dr Prasad.'

That was true. Supercute hired the best people and trusted them to do their work.

'I'd like you to rest for a few hours.'

'We have a board meeting.'

'You have time to rest. Aifu is handling all the advance preparations.'

'How do you know that?'

'Aifu told me. He doesn't want you straining yourselves.'

Mox turned her head towards Mitsu. 'He's always looking after us.'

'He does like to fuss.'

Aifu, named after the initials of his designation as Artificial Intelligence Forecast Unit, was a very important part of Supercute. A very important person, Mox and Mitsu would have said, though technically he was an android. A great deal of their business went through Aifu who now acted as chief executive, information centre, forecast specialist, financial data processor and, increasingly, their friend.

'That completes your skeletal upgrades. You're scheduled for more trapezius muscle enhancement in five weeks' time. Skin regeneration too, we've managed to improve UV resistance.'

'Don't we already have that?'

'Yes, but it can always be made better.'

'OK.'

'Have you given any more thought to my recommendation about your brains?' asked Dr Prasad.

'We're not that keen,' replied Mox.

'Why keep the organic thirty per cent?'

'It's the only original part we've got left.'

Dr Prasad sounded mildly disapproving. 'It's not doing you any good. Complete replacement would be more reliable.'

'We're worried we might lose our female intuition,' said Mitsu.

'You're well aware that's a non-scientific myth.'

'I know. But we'll keep the remnants of our original brains for now. We've done OK so far.'

Later, resting in their recovery room, on beds covered with a comforting multitude of soft cuddly toys, they smiled at Dr Prasad's words.

'She's a great doctor but she's awfully keen on replacing body parts.'

'You know she won't let it go.'

'Probably not. She's right, I suppose. Complete replacement would be more efficient. It's just . . .'

Mitsu didn't have to complete the sentence. They were now ninety-four per cent artificial and both shared a superstitious reluctance to go the whole way, to have every single part of their bodies made artificial. The organic brain parts they still possessed had been artificially regenerated several times, but they were still biologically human. With them gone, well . . . It wasn't something they were quite ready to do.

The lights dimmed and they slept for an hour.

*

Birgit waited politely for Amowie to invite her into her space, though she didn't really need to. They'd adjusted their Supatok settings so that no invitation was necessary. Birgit in Iceland, Amowie in Nigeria, Meihui in China and Raquel in Paraguay were in and out of each other's spaces all the time and it would have been tedious to keep asking for permission.

'Hello!'

'Come in!'

Birgit was a pale girl, the same age as Amowie, naturally blonde and blue eyed, though at this moment she had purple hair and purple eyes, modelled on Roota Space Warrior.

'I brought you the facemask pattern, you can use it here right now and you can print it too, if you want.'

'Thank you! I love Supercute facemasks!' Amowie touched her screen to Birgit's, accepting the information, then touched her screen again. Her nose and mouth were immediately covered by a pink facemask decorated by a picture of two cute little cupcakes.

'This is great! I'll save up to get one printed.'

'Don't you have your own printer?'

'No.'

'Well, it won't cost much to get some made.'

'Xaka at the village workshop will do it for me. He always laughs when I take him Supercute stuff but he does them for me cheap, free sometimes.'

Amowie liked Birgit. It was nice of her to bring her a spare facemask pattern. The masks, modelled on the medical gear worn by doctors, but cuter, were cheap downloads from Supercute but Amowie had very little money and couldn't afford her own. Most of her friends were wearing them in their own spaces these days, and when she visited them she'd been feeling left out. Amowie had many Supercute friends around the world and she met and talked to them often in Supatok. They swapped and gave each other merchandise, which Mox and Mitsu encouraged on the show, not minding swaps at all, apparently. That didn't mean things were free in the first place, or could easily be pirated. The quantum encryption used by MitsuMox Global Merchandise had never been broken, and anything which might be swapped or donated later had certainly been paid for at one time.

Mr Schulze had not been enjoying executive meetings. The tension brought on by RX Enviro's problems made them fraught affairs. Making the latest meeting worse, they were now watching the Moe Bennie show. He glared at the screen where Bennie and his youthful cohorts cavorted around what appeared to be a sub-tropical island, with palm trees and a chorus of pink, singing swordfish.

> '*It's Moe Bennie and the cuddle crew*
> *Moe Bennie and the cuddle crew*
> *Always bright and always new*
> *Moe Bennie and the cuddle crew!*'

It was a relief when Ms Mason switched it off. She turned to Mr Hernandez. 'It's well done, but it's not as good as Supercute.'

Mr Hernandez nodded. 'My kids don't like him.'

'I can't tell the difference,' said Mr Schulze.

'Really, Schulze?'

'Isn't it all just annoying youngsters in silly clothes?'

Ms Mason considered this. 'I wouldn't say so. It's the

transmission of emotion. Supercute project a human warmth that Moe Bennie can't match. Which is ironic, as I doubt either of the Supercute girls have a human molecule left in their bodies.'

Mason, Schulze and Hernandez between them could boast many discreet body enhancements though none were as extensively modified as Mox and Mitsu. Advanced bio-tech was not uncommon but the expense involved limited such procedures to the very wealthy. Millions of people around the world struggled on without it. Medicine may have progressed but for the majority of the population, life expectancy had decreased in the past eighty years.

'So,' continued Ms Mason. 'What about Lark 3's take-over plan?'

Mr Hernandez frowned. 'I just don't see how Moe Bennie can pull it off. I can believe he's got a tacit under-standing with C19, but Supercute Enterprises is such a huge conglomerate. Not just Supercute Entertainment, Supercute Communication and ZanZan Defence, they've got the desalinisation, the financial holdings, MitsuMox Global Merchandise ... How can he possibly bring them down?'

'He claims to have secret agreements with their investors which will give him twelve per cent of the company's shares.'

'How?'

'Presumably by means we don't want to know about,' said Ms Mason.

Mr Schulze smiled for the first time. 'Fraud and blackmail, no doubt. Murder too, wouldn't surprise me. I'll be keeping my mini-drones close if we have to do business with him.'

Neither Ms Mason nor Mr Hernandez was moved to contradict Mr Schulze. Rivalries among members of C19 were meant to be solved by peaceful means but violence did sometimes occur. When it came to members of C19 protecting their interests against lesser corporations trying to move up in the world, it was common.

'Even if he can get twelve per cent, so what?' Hernandez read some figures from a floating screen. 'The investors only hold forty per cent. Mox and Mitsu own sixty. They can't be outvoted. There's no way of making the company change hands. If we back Moe Bennie with three hundred billion it might destroy us.'

Ms Mason's looked pointedly at her subordinates. Her voice took on a harder edge. 'If we do nothing, we're facing destruction anyway. We can't survive Supercute ZanZan's move into Central America.'

Mox woke up feeling depressed after the procedure. It had been necessary to build their own advanced medical unit because she'd always had an aversion to hospitals. The fact that her first experience of hospital had been arriving there in an ambulance alongside her dead mother still made her wary of them. Even here, secure in Supercute headquarters, she didn't enjoy undergoing treatment. Mitsu woke up a few moments later and immediately picked up on her unhappiness.

'Don't worry, we only have to rest here a little longer.'

'We've got a big meeting, we should be getting ready. I'm getting up.'

Mox cleared away several cuddly toys, ready to pull back the *Blue Bronto and Dinosaur Friends Quilt* from her bed. At that moment Aifu entered the room.

'Stay right there, Ms Bennet. You have another twenty-three minutes' rest prescribed for you and you're not moving till it's over.'

'Ooh, Aifu, I want to get up.' Mox suddenly sounded like a child. Aifu came over to her bed. For an Artificial Intelligence Forecast Unit he was a very good-looking young man. Purposely styled for Supercute, he had dark shoulder-length hair, feline, slightly feminine features, large eyes and a lithe physique. Around his eyes were several small patches of silver metal, the only indication he wasn't human. He looked exactly like a manga hero, which had been the intention.

'Hi Aifu,' said Mitsu.

Aifu put his hand close to Mox's face, then did the same to Mitsu, taking readings. He nodded. 'The procedure went well. In twenty-two minutes you'll be back in action.'

'I hate waiting around like an invalid,' grumbled Mox.

'We do have nice new shoulders,' said Mitsu, cheerfully. 'Completes the upgrade. I'm feeling good.'

'I'm not.'

'Yes you are. You just like to complain.'

Mox laughed, cheered by Mitsu, and by Aifu's appearance. They were close to Aifu these days.

'I've completed all security checks for the transfer. You'll have a lot of money and shares changing hands, we don't want anything going wrong.'

'Is everything in order?'

'We're impregnable.'

'Good. We have confidence in you, Aifu.'

It was true. In the past two years, Supercute had channelled more and more of their business through Aifu. He'd proved to be extremely reliable. His Weyl fermion brain had outperformed their competitors and he'd brought them business advantages they'd never have accrued otherwise.

'Though we still think you could do with brightening up a bit,' said Mox.

Aifu always wore black.

'Are you sure we can't give you a nice colourful kimono?'

'No thank you.'

'We'll put you on the show – *artificial intelligence Supercute makeover.*'

As always, Aifu was good-humoured about this, but declined the offer.

Mitsu turned to Mox. 'I think he just likes black clothes because he's got a secret Goth thing going on.'

'Probably out clubbing every night with his AI groupies.'

Aifu raised his eyebrows. 'You know I'd never play around behind your backs. I'm dedicated to looking after you.'

'Aw Aifu, you're so sweet.'

'Sometimes we worry you'll go all robotic and stop liking us,' said Mox.

'I'm sure that won't happen. I have to go and prepare for the meeting now. You need to rest for another eighteen minutes.'

Mox made a face. 'I don't want to.'

'Doctor's orders,' said Aifu. Mox resigned herself to waiting another eighteen minutes, which she wouldn't have done for anyone except Aifu. After he left, she picked up a fluffy dinosaur toy for comfort.

'I like our Artificial Intelligence Forecast Unit,' said Mitsu.

'You *love* him.'

'*You* love him.'

'You *super* love him.'

'You *extra* super love him.'

They both laughed.

'We're back to being six years old.' Mitsu looked thoughtful. 'Seriously, is it worrying that our artificial intelligence is probably our only real friend these days?'

Mox shrugged. 'I don't know. I suppose it's lonely at the top. But we never had that many friends. Even when we were young, people just thought we were strange.'

Castle trudged wearily into his flat in Elephant and Castle Emergency High Rise Block 14 and was disgusted to find the *Supercute Show* on the screen in the living room.

'Didn't I tell you never to show that?' he muttered. He had, but his entertainment hub was old, malfunctioning, and often misunderstood his instructions.

'Change it.'

'What to?' asked his entertainment hub.

'Anything that doesn't involve the bloody Supercute Girls.'

The channel changed to a sports station he could live with. He flung his coat on a chair. He opened the hallway cupboard that served as a drinks cabinet. Inside were four bottles of gin, two of them empty. He made a mental note to replenish his supply. He was about to pour himself a glass, neat, when he paused. He'd completed a case, tracking down a missing daughter, separating her from a particularly violent boyfriend and reuniting her with a grateful mother. Not only that, he'd been paid. That was fairly rare these days. Perhaps it deserved something better than cheap unadulterated gin.

'Are there any mixers anywhere?' he said, loudly.

His home assistant replied from one of the tiny speakers in the ceiling. 'You have lime juice in the fridge and concentrated orange juice in the next cupboard. The orange juice has probably gone bad by now.'

Castle took his glass of gin to the kitchen, mixed in some lime juice and then, with difficulty, extracted a tray of ice cubes from the freezer which, once again, had allowed itself to become clogged with ice instead of cleaning itself as it should have.

'These things never went wrong in the adverts,' he thought, remembering back to a time when automated computerised kitchen and home help was just being introduced. He took his drink to the living room and sat on the couch, an old piece of furniture that had been supplied when the high rise was built, an emergency dwelling for London's homeless after the Thames Estuary radiation disaster. It should have been cleared away by now, the inhabitants housed in fine new buildings somewhere else. That had never happened, and didn't ever seem likely to.

He put his feet up and watched the sports channel for a minute or so.

'Show me something else.'

'What would you like?'

'Anything as long as it's not bloody Supercute.'

Aifu waited patiently while Mox and Mitsu finished their make-up. Some of this was done by drones but they often finished the work off themselves. The drones, now hovering in the background, lacked the finesse necessary for the most specialised tasks. Blending four different pastel shades of eye-shadow into a perfect gradient could only be done by hand.

When they were ready, Aifu opened up the Supercute boardroom space in an arid desert. Mox and Mitsu walked in after him. For this important meeting they were dressed in their Supercute business suits, from the *Girls Fun Work*

Party range. Coloured in Supercute peach 8, Supercute blue 16 and Supercute pink 19, they bore little relation to anyone else's business suits, but they made the pair feel quite business-like. Another boardroom opened up in front of them, this one looking much like any real-life boardroom. Inside was Mr Salisbury, CEO of ZanZan Defence. Behind him were two smartly dressed executives and ZanZan's AIFU. Friendly greetings were exchanged. Friendly, because while linking up with ZanZan had been a business decision, in which they'd be senior partners, they liked Mr Salisbury. There was a moment's silence while Aifu and ZanZan's AIFU faced each other, exchanging financial information, the exchange taking place by way of optical transmission. Their eyes flickered as the data was exchanged and processed. It didn't take long.

'Is everything ready, Mr Salisbury?' asked Mox.

'Everything's in place. We'll be signing the attack drone contract in fourteen hours.' Mr Salisbury was soberly dressed and looked old-fashioned, the conservative cut of his suit being favoured by only the most traditional of businessmen these days. Mox and Mitsu liked that. It seemed appropriate for the CEO of a weapons company. They wouldn't have liked him to be jolly.

'The board have asked me to thank you for your work, Ms Inamura, Ms Bennet.'

'It's a good arrangement all round, Mr Salisbury,' said Mox. 'ZanZan Defence is a fine company. We have a bright future together.'

Mitsu took a step forward. 'We brought you the new Supercute laser assault satellite cuddly toy. You can download a copy for Jack.'

Mr Salisbury's face lit up. 'Thank you! Jack will love

this. He really loves you both, can't drag him away from the screen when you're on.'

Aifu interrupted them with an announcement. 'Supercute Greenfield.'

More boardrooms began to open up in front of them, each in its own space. There was a beach, a yacht, the moon, another traditional office, a mountain villa, all containing senior members of the boards of Supercute's main subsidiaries. While generally sober in tone, there were examples of Supercute merchandise in all of them, mascots, posters, bags and more. As each room opened Aifu announced their arrival.

'Supercute Communications. Mokusei Space Transit. Supercute Mokusei Financial Holdings. MitsuMox Global Merchandise . . .'

There were friendly greetings though the general air was one of respect towards Mox and Mitsu as bosses of the conglomerate. There was a little business talk, not that much. All preparations had been thoroughly examined and agreed beforehand and this meeting was mainly to confirm in everyone's presence that the acquisition of ZanZan was going ahead as planned, and everything was running smoothly. Mox and Mitsu trusted their executives to run their businesses but didn't like to appear distant. When important deals were being done they wanted to show they were personally involved.

Finally Mox asked if there were any remaining problems. The general reply was that no, there weren't, but Ms Barbosa from Supercute Mokusei Financial Holdings did raise a question. 'Is it true that Moe Bennie and Lark 3 held talks with your investors, the Laing DF group?'

Mox and Mitsu laughed. 'They *attempted* to hold talks.

God knows why. Laing sent them packing. I wouldn't worry about them, Ms Barbosa.'

Amowie and Birgit, who lived 6,500 kilometres apart, had found themselves confronted by the same problem. Neither of their parents approved of their Supercute obsessions.

It's not really a suitable style for wearing in Iceland.
It's not really a suitable style for wearing in Nigeria.

Mystified as to why their parents could be so hopelessly wrong about everything, Amowie and Birgit did their best to ignore their objections. It was a common phenomenon, after all. Their friend Tess's parents in Australia said exactly the same thing, and Meihui's mother in China was already warning her that if she kept on wearing her ridiculous Supercute outfits, she'd never find either a husband or a job. As Meihui was currently living in the Wudalianchi Volcano Disaster Relocation Camp, where jobs were not available and husbands were not uppermost in any of the survivors' minds, it seemed like an unnecessary thing to worry about, for the moment anyway.

Amowie and Birgit were both doing school projects on Supercute. Their teachers were not as averse to the subject as their parents, though they hadn't been overly enthusiastic either. Miss Bree had suggested to Amowie that here in Igboland there were many people, clothes, festivals and traditions of interest, all suitable subjects for her project. Miss Bree was quite passionate about Igboland. Amowie liked it too, but not so much that she'd pick it as a subject over Supercute.

She sat with Birgit in her personal space, taking clips of their favourite moments from the show and splicing them together. They'd been making good progress. Amowie couldn't wait to show her class their results. Not only would Miss Bree be impressed, it would quieten those detractors among her classmates who didn't like Mox and Mitsu. Even better, it might shut Ifunanya up. Ifunanya lived in the next village and was in the class above Amowie at school. Her family was one of the wealthiest in the area. She was always bragging about all the Supercute merchandise she'd bought, bringing things into school to show them off like she was the biggest Supercute fan in Igboland. Amowie, actually the biggest Supercute fan in Igboland, couldn't compete with her expenditure but there were other ways of demonstrating her superior fan status, one of which was her current school project.

'This is going to be great!'

A cloud of tiny pink Supercute eems hovered around them. The little spheres were smiling, positively affected by Amowie's optimism. Supercute eems were much better than anyone else's and they gave you hundreds of them free when you watched their show.

'Let's try that part,' said Birgit. They were attempting to animate a news story they'd found during their research.

'*Ms Inamura Mitsu and Ms Mox Bennet, proprietors of Supercute, are seen here donating a solid gold bar, weighing 400 Troy ounces (12.4 kg) to help with the restoration of the Wat Traimit temple in Bangkok, which was severely damaged by the recent tsunami ...*'

They only had a few photographs of the event, which they were attempting to make into a realistic animated hologram, but the programming involved in turning such meagre sources into good 3-D animation was quite advanced and they were struggling to get it right. Examining their latest attempt, they were disappointed.

The Supercute eems turned a disillusioned green and sank towards the floor.

'We could ask Connor for help. He's good at this sort of thing.'

Amowie made a face. 'Connor? I'm still mad at him.'

Connor, a Supercute friend of theirs in Australia, had recently mocked them for sneaking into a part of Supercute Fairy Realm that was meant to be reserved for children. Amowie was still a little embarrassed about it.

'I just wanted to try their new wings. No neeed for him to be mean.'

'He was just annoyed because we didn't take him. How about Raquel? Let's ask her.'

Raquel in Paraguay had very advanced computing skills.

'I'm not asking her for help unless she admits that Moe Bennie's hair is the worst hair ever.'

They laughed. Amowie and Birgit hated Moe Bennie. They'd been shocked to learn that Raquel, a fellow Supercute fan, actually thought he had nice hair. Foolishness like that had to be eradicated, for Raquel's own good.

Lark 3 Media's Artificial Intelligence Forecast Unit had been christened Igraine by Moe Bennie. In style she was similar to Supercute's AIFU. She appeared young, attractive, pale-skinned, dark-haired, and wore a black jumpsuit. She looked mostly human, only a few subtle metallic features revealing her true nature. Moe Bennie did not regard her with the same affection as Mox and Mitsu showed towards Aifu, but he did value her. They were often in each other's company at work. She stood by his side as he made the connection to talk to RX Enviro's board.

'Ms Mason. Did you enjoy my show?'

'No,' said RX Enviro's CEO. 'Our children prefer Supercute.'

Moe Bennie immediately became angry and struggled to reign in his temper. 'Supercute are talentless hacks who should have retired thirty years ago! If we're going into partnership I don't think you should be saying—'

'We're not partners yet, Mr Bennie.'

There was an awkward silence, broken by Igraine. 'You asked for further information, Ms Mason?'

'We want to know how you can take over Supercute with only twelve per cent of their shares.'

'Twelve per cent is a necessary start. When we reach that figure, it will automatically trigger Supercute's financial defences.'

'And that's a good thing?'

'At that figure, their AIFU will start producing options to buy voting shares.'

'Why? Ms Bennet and Ms Inamura own sixty per cent of the shares already, they can't be outvoted.'

'Indeed they cannot. The defence mechanism exists only to protect them in the unlikely event of all the other shareholders voting against them in certain matters of company organisation. According to their rules, sixty-five per cent of shareholder votes are required for certain structural alterations in the company. Acquiring ZanZan, for instance, requires them to move Mokusei Space Transit's company registration from France to Switzerland. In practice there's no chance of the other shareholders opposing them, but if it were to happen that an attempt was made to buy the required amount of shares to hinder their restructuring, more shares would automatically be offered to Ms Bennet and Ms Inamura. These shares will be produced automatically when their financial defences detect the possibly hostile acquisition of twelve per cent of the current total. Once these options are triggered, we plan to buy them.'

'But you can't,' said Mr Hernandez. 'They'll only be offered to Bennet and Inamura.'

Igraine rarely showed emotion. She was capable of it, but not yet experienced in its use. In this instance, she smiled very faintly. 'We can. All their transactions are now managed by their AIFU. I have successfully hacked this AIFU. I can control it.'

Mox, alone with Aifu in her office suite, leaned back against him, and gazed at the wall. It was covered in framed photographs, a small selection from their collection of contemporary Scandinavian photography. In the next office was part of their collection of Japanese theatrical posters, mainly Shakespearean. Along the corridor in Sachi's office there was a painting by Sir Frederic Leighton, part of their collection of Victorian and Pre-Raphaelite art, most of which was on loan to Tate Ten. Mox and Mitsu owned several more art collections, all carefully curated, some displayed at their headquarters, some in their London and New Tokyo residences, and some loaned to galleries.

'Aifu, I need a few minutes, can you keep everyone away?'

'Of course.'

'Thank you.'

Mox's visor appeared over her eyes and she moved into her therapy space. Her therapist greeted her in his calm, reassuring manner.

'We didn't start off as entertainment for the masses. Supercute never meant superbland. Mainly we were showing off our cute clothes and playing with our favourite toys, but right from the start we had other parts in the show. We supported women's rights all around the world. We mocked and satirised people we didn't like. And not just easy targets. Back in those days if you ridiculed some right-wing politician people would applaud like you were great. We did that, quite a lot. But we mocked other people too. Even minorities sometimes, which was a taboo thing to do. We did that just to annoy people. It was funny. Got us a surprising amount of attention. People demanding we apologised. We never did. We just told everyone to go fuck themselves, and kept on going.

'We used to brag about our degrees and our PhDs which was an unusual thing for young girls to do. If people didn't like it, to hell with them. We didn't care what people thought. And we always featured science on the show, and maths. A lot of education.'

Mox paused, and was thoughtful for a while.

'It turned out no one much cared for education. It got less as the show got bigger. Same with the outrages. Advertisers didn't like outrages, and by then we were earning a lot of money from advertising. So then we were just entertainment. Though after the impacts, the endless winter, the wars, the long drought, the depression, just being entertainment didn't seem so bad, really. Most people were having such a hard time it felt good to be able to entertain them. By this time we were the biggest show in the world. We were popular in just about every country. We spoke so many languages, we'd be working day and night preparing versions for every territory. If we didn't speak the language we'd use subtitles and dubbing till there was nowhere we weren't popular. We started off with an iPhone in a bedroom and ended up with weekly viewing figures as big as the Olympic Games, when there still were Olympic Games. It was quite a phenomenon. It still is.'

Mox paused again. 'Then we discovered something we hadn't known before. When you get to a certain size, you can't stop.'

'What do you mean?'

'When your business is that big, you can't stay still. You need investors and they want growth. If you don't keep growing, someone will come along and swallow you up.'

While most educational aspects had long since disappeared from the *Supercute Show*, there were still occasional expositions on popular science topics, briefly explained in simple terms by Happy Little Science Pixie. But for Mox and Mitsu, who'd once stood in front of their iPhone camera, dressed in their cutest outfits, each holding a cuddly panda toy, confidently and accurately explaining to their viewers that a recent claim to have solved the Manin conjecture was wrong, and the equation

$$N_{U,H}(B) = \#\{x \in U(K) : H(x) \leqq B\}$$

had not yet been proven to be true for all the required conditions, Happy Little Science Pixie was always something of a disappointment.

Amowie and Birgit, working on the school projects, wouldn't have agreed. Happy Little Science Pixie was better than nothing, and a lot more informative that anything their rivals did. They were keen to stress this to their teachers while listing the various benefits that Supercute had brought to the world.

'Supercute has partnerships with museums in every continent, and encourages their audience to visit their virtual exhibitions!

Supercute language courses have been used by millions of people. And the Supercute instant translator is much better than the other boring ones on the market!

In the Supercute coding instructor, Mox and Mitsu sit right beside you and show you how to get started! It's the most popular coding instructor for under-14s in the world!'

Amowie and Birgit thought that was a good start. They were still adding to their list of all Supercute's acts of charity, of which there were many, intending to build up an overwhelmingly positive image.

'We have to mention the free clothes.'

Most visitors to Supercute space had their own garments, some owning a very extensive range. But for anyone there for the first time, or entirely without funds, a free basic kit was provided. Even if you had no money, or weren't sure what to wear when you got there, as soon as you entered any Supercute Fun World you'd find yourself in something pretty, something suitable, something cute. It was a part of the service, one that Amowie in particular had appreciated. These days she had her own garments but when she'd first entered Supercute space to watch the show she hadn't had any. Immediately she'd found herself dressed in an outfit that fitted in perfectly with everyone else. It meant that no one was ever left out. Amowie felt an enduring warmth towards Mox and Mitsu for that.

It was Mox and Mitsu's skills in designing cute, colourful clothes that had driven the huge expansion in their merchandising. Their garments were quirky, pretty, colour-ful, original, sometimes juvenile, and sometimes, for their older fans, subtly erotic. Many were unisex, creating an army of androgynous fans around the world, often dressed in styles influenced not just by Mox and Mitsu's memories of their friends in Tokyo, but also by their unusual knowl-edge of British glam rock, a twentieth-century phenomenon now long forgotten, except by them. Very few people these days would have recognised Marc Bolan: Mox and Mitsu had posters of him on their walls.

Supercute clothes were mostly inexpensive. They might also be said to be, on occasion, educational. Amowie enthusiastically added additional commentary to their soundtrack. 'The *Blue Bronto* T-shirt features a back-ground of the complete evolutionary tree of life!'

Birgit joined in. 'My Shanina Space Warrior T-shirt shows her wielding her antiproton sword over a back-ground of Maxwell's equations!'

'And there's Superpink Superbunny. Here she's sitting right on top of the ancient Acropolis, accurately depicted.'

Mox and Mitsu retained these images merely as a design quirk. They were under no illusions that fans of Shanina Space Warrior, on purchasing the T-shirt, were liable to feel an urge to study Maxwell's ground-breaking differential equations, no matter how important they'd been to the foundation of classical electrodynamics. Amowie and Birgit thought it was worth pointing out to their teachers anyway, just in case they thought Supercute were not worthy of a school project. They were very worthy, and Amowie and Brigit carried on adding as much as they could to make their projects successful.

*

There was scepticism in the boardroom of RX Enviro. Ms Mason found Igraine's claim hard to believe.

'You're saying you can control Supercute's AIFU?'

'Yes.'

'How?'

'Every AIFU is customised uniquely for their employer but they do still share a certain amount of base quantum hardware and software. I've discovered a flaw in their AIFU's quantum key distribution, resulting, I believe, from a missed or improperly applied upgrade. Using this flaw I'm now able to take control.'

'Supposing that's true, is controlling one artificial intelligence enough to take over a company the size of Supercute?'

'Their AIFU has an unusual degree of control of their affairs. Far more than might be expected. Ms Bennet and Ms Inamura seem to trust it with everything. It's an error on their part.'

Moe Bennie leaned forward eagerly. 'We can make their AIFU trigger the share sale then force him to sell to us. In the space of a few minutes, we'll be able to gain a majority shareholding, freeze their accounts, cut off their communications, disable their defences and take complete control.'

'They're not going to walk out of that building without a fight,' said Mr Hernandez.

'We're planning to arrive when they're otherwise occupied. Approximately fifteen minutes after we make our move, Ms Mox Bennet and Ms Inamura Mitsu are going to find themselves out on the streets, with nothing. You'll take the desalinisation and environment business, ZanZan Defence will be split up and sold, and I'll take over Supercute Entertainment and Communications.'

There was a long pause while the chief executives of RX

Enviro considered Moe Bennie's proposition. The stars shone overhead and a large moon hung low in the sky.

'We'll need to see proof that you can really control their AIFU. Physical proof, not just numbers.'

'Of course, Ms Mason.' Igraine brought up a screen which showed Aifu standing next to Mox while she applied her make-up.

'Choose a finger.'

'Left index.'

Igraine brought up her personal screen, a small transparent rectangle which projected from her left wrist, and tapped in a few commands. As they watched, Supercute's AIFU moved his left index finger, as instructed.

Moe Bennie was triumphant. 'We're going to destroy them.'

Mitsu strode into the dressing room to find Marlene, one of their young designers, standing next to a life-size Mitsu hologram. Marlene was working on new outfits for the show. She smiled at Mitsu but was alarmed to see her employer scowling.

'What the fuck is that?'

'Eh . . . I added more face paint, like you asked.'

Mox and Mitsu were keen face-painters, sometimes doing segments of their show with quite extravagant designs, the general theme of which was robotic warpaint.

'Not that – I mean that!' Mitsu pointed angrily to the hologram's knee-length socks. 'Did you just decide to ignore the Supercute Style Manual?'

Their style manual specified that any socks or stockings had to extend to an area just four centimetres below the hem of whatever skirts or shorts Mox and Mitsu were wearing, the only exceptions being the short ankle socks they sometimes wore with Japanese sandals, and the children's designs used in Supercute Fairy Realm.

'Sorry, Ms Inamura. I'll see to it right away.'

Marlene hurried off to reprogram her design. Moments later Mox appeared in the dressing room. She reeled in shock when she saw the hologram.

'What the fuck is that?'

'It's OK, I've dealt with it.'

'How could our designers do something so terrible?'

'Well, she's normally good,' said Mitsu, charitably. Mox nodded. Marlene was a good clothes designer. They wouldn't hold one error against her.

Sachi's voice sounded from a tiny speaker in the wall. 'Ladies, we need a few voiceovers.'

'Send them down,' said Mitsu.

A screen materialised in front of them. They read from it while Sachi talked to them from her director's booth upstairs.

'Comedy English, one.'

Mox adopted the thickest of London cockney accents. *'Cor blimey, it's them supacute gels, guv'nor!'*

'Comedy English, two.'

Mox adopted an exaggerated English upper-class accent, which was not too far removed from the way she sounded much of the time, in private. *'One endeavours never to miss an episode of their splendid programme!'*

'Good. Now comedy Japanese, one.'

Mitsu did her lines, creating similar effects in Japanese, first using highly formal language, followed by an exaggeratedly oafish regional accent.

'Thank you, Mitsu.'

46

'Do you want some funny English from me?'

'Don't you dare!' cried Sachi, and ended the conversation.

Mox laughed. Mitsu's purposeful mispronunciation of several English words had once been one of their favourite ploys for causing outrage. Asian Americans seemed to find it particularly offensive, and complained in numbers. Complaints had always led to increased viewing figures.

'It's a shame we can't annoy people like that any more. Not without losing global advertising deals, anyway.'

A small rotating holograph in the corner of the room caught Mox's eye; a silver-haired woman carrying a huge sword.

'Remember how much we used to love Claymore?'

'First cosplay outfits we ever made. With the big cardboard swords covered with silver paper.'

'We used to run around your garden fighting monsters. Completely destroyed the flowerbeds.'

Mitsu smiled. 'My mum was nice about it. She always was understanding.'

Castle lived on the tenth floor though it would have been hard to tell from inside his flat. The self-cleaning windows in the high rise had not self-cleaned for several years and were covered with thick layers of grime. The rain cleared away some of it but these days London went for months at a time without rain. The whole place was untidy. The small robot-vacuum assigned to each flat had disappeared with the previous tenant and Castle had never felt inclined to do its work. His apartment might be messy but it was comfortable enough. In the army he'd coped with much worse. He didn't really mind living in such a poor area though it was a reminder of how badly his career had gone. Lying on the couch, he touched his wrist, causing an electronic business card to appear.

Benjamin Castle, Private Investigator.

'Generally available due to lack of work,' he muttered, and shook his head. Things hadn't been so bad last year when he'd worked for a large agency with an address in Mayfair, but the organisation had gone under, victim to a scandal in which the head of the agency was found to have been taking bribes to fake evidence. Castle had been surprised; he'd thought they were honest, which was naïve of him. Since then, he'd worked on his own but had never managed to garner much of a clientele. He had managed to drink a lot of gin.

Before the agency ... He scowled. Before the agency he'd been very well paid. The effects of that were still with him, if not visible in his surroundings. He'd had a lot of internal enhancements, major biotech improvements to his physique. With his military and investigating skills, and his upgraded frame, he should have been a valued operator, capable of working in any circumstances. Yet here he was lying on the couch in a shabby old flat, drinking gin.

'Bloody Supercute,' he muttered. 'I blame them for everything. And Ishikawa. I blame her too. But mainly Supercute.'

Supercute were mistresses of communication. Their commitment to reaching a worldwide audience had been an important part of their rise to dominance. Before the age of instant translators they'd always attempted to make their show available in as many languages as possible. Even in the early days of their career, with sections rerecorded in all the languages they spoke, and other parts dubbed or subtitled, there were few people around the world who couldn't watch a version of the show in a language they could understand. At first they brought in student friends to help them and when the show expanded they hired specialist support. No one else had ever made such efforts and it brought them their first devoted following. Later they'd pioneered the use of instant translators, pouring in resources while their rivals failed to keep up. By the time the programme moved fully into Supercute virtual space they were world leaders in translation technology. Anyone around the world could enter their space and find the whole show instantly and accurately interpreted into their native language. Words, phrases, colloquialisms, jokes, metaphors, alliteration, figures of speech, everything was perfectly translated by Supercute's own advanced artificial intelligence so that no one was left out. Supercute became the first show that could accurately claim a regular mass global audience.

When they'd attracted the attention of the world's youth, something happened they hadn't expected. They also attracted the attention of the world's leaders. If the World Health Authority needed to broadcast an emergency health warning or UNESCO desperately required aid, they came to Supercute, pleading for airtime. If you could somehow get Supercute to support your cause, it gained more attention than anything else could. Other world leaders, some with less worthy aims, also made overtures. Supercute resisted all political involvement for a long time but it was political pressure which eventually led to them becoming members of C19. With so much wealth, power and influence, they couldn't avoid it.

Their Roman villa stood some way south of Supercute's headquarters on land they owned. Thanks to Mox and

Mitsu it had been beautifully restored. Every floor had been uncovered and cleaned, revealing some fine mosaics and an almost intact bathing room. There were remnants of the heating system where hot water had been pumped through underfloor lead pipes, and most of one wall was still standing after two thousand years of burial. There was a small collection of Roman coins, many pottery shards, and an exquisite silver bracelet, one of the finest pieces of Roman jewellery ever found in Britain. The excavation and preservation had been paid for entirely by Supercute. There was no public funding available for archaeology.

Mox and Mitsu stood under the shade of a huge umbrella while the technical crew made ready for their broadcast. Mox was very pale-skinned; without the improved UV protection provided by her biotech, she'd have suffered badly from the relentless sun. She gazed at the mural underfoot: Poseidon holding a trident.

'Doing the show from this Roman villa just depresses me these days.'

'It's still a beautiful setting.'

'I know. But it's like the last pathetic remnants of our hopeless attempts at public education. *Kids, check out the ancient buildings near you.* When did the world just give up on learning?'

Mitsu shrugged. 'Probably around Plato's time. I expect his students were more interested in chariot racing than the theory of forms.'

Southwest of the villa were several poorly built areas of housing which tailed off into an unrestored stretch of baked mud and rubble. London had not suffered a great amount of war damage, most of that being in Central Europe, but flooding had been very extensive. Equally destructive were the uncontrollable fires that followed. After that there was a long period of civil disturbance. Large parts of the city and its suburbs were still desolate, some so badly damaged that there were currently no plans for renovation.

'I liked when we brought the fairies here,' said Mitsu. 'But it never really caught on.'

'No. Everyone liked Fairy Space Forest much better.'

Supercute Fairy Realm was a very popular part of their empire. Designed for children, it allowed users to fly around on fairy wings in a fantastic, magical reality. Making this completely realistic had required vast amounts of money and some advances in the science of aerodynamics. It had also led to advances in security, with new developments in long-range biometrics being required to keep adults out. They'd based their fairy designs on the Flower Fairies, created by Cicely Mary Barker in 1920, ancient now. Supercute owned the copyright and their fairies remained, as they had started out, very English.

'Are we going to do the *doujinshi* segment?'

Mitsu frowned. 'Do we feel like arguing with marketing again?'

Mox and Mitsu owned an extensive collection of Supercute *doujinshi*: comics, either paper, digital or holographic, self-published by fans. Some of these were well-made, some were poor and some were pornographic, mixing up imaginary tales of Mox and Mitsu with the cast from *Supercute Space Warriors* and other characters from the Supercute universe. Their marketing department would have liked all of these sued and banned. Mox and Mitsu themselves took a more relaxed attitude, leaving them to function undisturbed apart from the most pornographic or derogatory.

51

'Last time we praised any *doujinshi*, marketing almost went into meltdown. They're convinced that if some kid in Malaysia is allowed to draw a comic about us it'll cost us millions in royalties.'

'Well, I suppose that's what we employ them for.'

They looked south to where they could see the tops of the tall buildings in the financial centre at the Wharf, blue-tinged from the electronic shielding protecting them. Their marketing department owned a tower there, next to one owned by Supercute Mokusei Financial Holdings. That part of the city was functioning well but around it were several deep trenches that were little more than swampland; flooding had caused the ground to collapse into the sewers and tunnels below. While excavating at the villa they'd discovered several derelict tunnels, some dug for the Tube network, some much older. They were interesting, particularly one old watercourse which flowed right beneath their headquarters, but exploration was mostly impossible due to high levels of radiation.

Sachi appeared, two assistants behind her, a few tiny camera drones above. Mitsu complimented her suit. Their director always wore dark suits. Today's was black, with a blue shirt and black tie. Mox and Mitsu admired her determined conservatism.

'There's an air cleanser in shot,' said Sachi. These tall white tubes surrounded the villa, removing pollution from the air, creating a localised clean spot. Her assistant hurriedly repositioned Mox and Mitsu so that the cleanser couldn't be seen.

'Ninety seconds, ladies.'

Before the show, adverts played.

'Pretty Blush Cat sits beside you and give you precise

instructions for your super-big eyes, lipstick, lip gloss, foundation, eye shadow, eye liner, everything. No need to reapply – Pretty Blush Cat automatically transfers your current make-up into your space for that perfect Supercute look.'

The advert segued into their theme music. Three small cameras hovered towards Mox and Mitsu. Their demeanour transformed, their slight depression vanishing. When they presented the show they were bright, cheerful and energetic. They'd never been anything less, even if they needed to dose themselves with fern three to replenish their energy. That was rare though it had been happening more frequently recently.

'*Space Warriors* intro.'

In front of the camera Mox burst into life. '*Supercute Space Warriors!*'

Mitsu was similarly energised. 'We love these warriors!'

'And we have a new episode right now!'

Their audience found themselves transported into the fully realised Space Warriors universe, travelling along with them on their adventures. They shared the experience of the stars going dim as the warriors soared through the galaxy, faster than light, in pursuit of the evil Krogdar mercenaries.

Mox and Mitsu watched, without paying much attention.

'How many times have we explained why you can't actually travel faster than light?' wondered Mitsu.

'About a thousand. People still never get it. I don't know why, it's not that bloody hard to understand.'

'Maybe we shouldn't have dropped our science segments.'

'What could we do? The advertisers were starting to complain.'

They checked their appearance before the episode ended. Bernard from make-up fussed over Mitsu's face paint, not being quite satisfied with one of the light blue stripes on her cheek. She didn't protest. It had to be perfect.

Sachi's voice sounded on the set. 'Space Warriors game segment.'

Mox spread her arms expansively as she spoke to the camera. 'Remember, *Supercute Space Warriors* nine is now on sale!'

'Top of the gaming charts for thirty-six weeks! Fight your way through the greatest galaxy ever!'

'Want to meet some of the characters? Here they are—'

'The Supercute Space Warriors!' cried Mitsu.

Characters from the game appeared. They strode around the villa, realistic, colourful, long hair in blue and pink and yellow, manga superheroes with added Supercute styling. They were by far the best-looking and most colourful space heroes around, in a genre with a lot of competition. They had the best clothes and the best stories. Supercute were diligent about hiring the most talented writers for both the game and the animation. Last year's romance between Roota Space Warrior and Jax the Astronomer-Poet had won a Golden Globe for *Best Storyline Involving Non-Humans*.

'Banking Girl segment.'

Holographic money showered down over Mox and Mitsu. Mitsu reacted with great excitement.

'What's this?'

'It's Banking Girl!' cried Mox.

Banking Girl danced onto the scene, the very cute mascot of Supercute Financial Holdings. She burst into song.

'I'm super-cute and super-funny
I look after your parents' money!
Nice safe banking every day!
Supercute Finance leads the way!'

'Thanks, Banking Girl!' said Mox.

'Do you have any super offers for us this week?' asked Mitsu.

Banking Girl beamed at them. 'Of course! I—'

Banking Girl abruptly disappeared. Mox and Mitsu looked towards Sachi.

'Technical hitch ladies, keep going.'

Professional, unperturbed by a slight production problem, Mox and Mitsu smiled at their audience.

'We've got a technical problem! Don't worry, that sometimes happens in Supercute World!'

'So let's go and see what the Supercute kids are up to in Rio.'

There was a pause. Nothing happened.

'Where's Rio?' asked Mitsu, still smiling.

'We appear to have lost everything.' Sachi's voice sounded in their ears. It was followed immediately by an urgent transmission from Aifu.

'Mox, Mitsu, we have a problem. You need to get back here.'

Mox looked towards Sachi. 'Run the reserve episode of Supercute Space Warriors. Aifu, what's happening?'

'We're under attack.'

'What do you mean?'

'Marlon Premium just sold all their Supercute shares to Lark 3.'

'What?' Mitsu was startled. 'Has old Marlon finally gone mad?'

'Marlon is dead. Car crash. His son took over this morning.'

'So his son's a moron. Can you deal with it, Aifu? We've got a show to do.'

'Marlon isn't the only problem. Laing are selling too. The—' There was a brief crackling sound as Aifu's line went dead.

'Sachi, what's going on?'

'Aifu's gone silent. I can't connect to headquarters.'

'Route the call through our satellite.'

'Supercute satellite has gone dark too.'

Mox and Mitsu looked at each other.

'We need to get back there.'

Three large valocopters flew towards Supercute headquarters. The engines made little noise and the rotors had been designed for stealth. A small Moe Bennie logo had been hastily stuck onto each neutral grey fuselage. Inside the leading craft Moe Bennie sat with a screen hovering over his lap. Beside him was Igraine. Also in the multicopter were Mr Jansen, Lark 3 Media's Chief Financial Officer, Ms Lesuuda, their security chief, and Mr Pham, Head of Cyber Strategy.

Igraine spoke softly to Moe Bennie, the low volume of the engines and the insulation of the passenger area making it unnecessary to shout. 'Our share purchase has triggered the production of emergency voting shares. I'm diverting them to Lark 3 Media.'

Moe Bennie read from his screen. 'Eighteen per cent ... Mr Pham, are their electronic communications completely jammed?'

'Yes, Mr Bennie. I've isolated their hub. They can't use their space. Nor their satellite.'

'What about their emergency reserve force?'

'Also isolated. They wont realise anything's wrong until it's too late.'

'Good.' Moe Bennie had plans in place for the Supercute guards in their headquarters but was concerned about the emergency force housed in properties to the south. Ostensibly security guards, they were actually reserve armed troops. If they were warned about what was happening before Moe Bennie was able to seize the building, they could end up in a full-scale battle.

'Twenty-two per cent ... Ms Lesuuda, the moment we reach fifty-one per cent we'll be going inside. I want your troops deployed and drones in the air within thirty seconds.'

'Yes, Mr Bennie.'

'Twenty-nine per cent ... Igraine, is there any sign of Supercute's secondary financial defences?'

'Emergency signals from their financial centres in Bern and Hong Kong. We're blocking them.'

Igraine's eyes flickered as she continued to wield control over Supercute's AIFU, simultaneously assisting Mr Pham with his cyber warfare. She was an immensely powerful unit, as they were all coming to realise.

'Is there any sign of police presence?'

'None so far.'

Moe Bennie judged that the police would be unlikely to become involved in a private squabble between members of C19 on land owned by Supercute. Supercute were licensed to police it themselves, and if another member of C19 decided to invade, that was generally regarded as their own business. Nonetheless, Mr Jansen, Financial Officer, had been in touch with the Chief Constable responsible for the nearest non-privately policed land, to make an arrangement, just in case.

Mox and Mitsu raced towards their headquarters. Sachi drove, overriding the autodriver which wouldn't go fast enough. Mox attempted to contact Aifu through the tiny mouthpiece which flickered on and off at her command.

'Aifu? Where are you? Aifu?' She turned to Mitsu. 'Nothing. I'll try his space.' A holovisor appeared and dropped over her eyes. She attempted to enter Aifu's space, which should have been easy, but found her way blocked by a type of electronic barrier she'd never encountered before. She snapped back to reality, dismissing her visor.

'No use. His space is blocked off.'

Sachi raced through the streets, delayed at times by traffic, though not as much as she once would have been. Traffic was much less than it had been thirty years ago. They reached the reserved business route that ran past the Wharf to Barking, a private motorway, well-maintained, shielded from the desolation on either side. Here they could make faster progress. The car windows dimmed a little, protection from the burning sun which shone fiercely on the exposed road.

Mitsu was studying her own screen. 'We just got an emergency alert from Bern. It was cut off. I'll go check.' Mitsu's visor came down and she entered the space maintained by their financial centre in Bern in Switzerland. There she was greeted by a frantic executive.

'Ms Inamura! We've been trying to contact you. Lark 3 are buying up your shares!'

'What do you mean?'

'They've triggered your automatic defences so your AIFU is producing more voting shares. But they're not going to you, they're going to them!'

'That's impossible.'

'I know! But it's happening. Look, they're up to thirty-five per cent!'

Mitsu glanced at the figures. In the car, her visor vanished as she turned to Mox. 'We're under attack. Moe Bennie's buying up voting shares.'

'No one can buy our voting shares.'

'They can, and they're creating more. They're up to thirty-five per cent.'

Mox screwed up her face. 'Aifu can't let this happen. It's impossible.'

Mitsu's earpiece buzzed. 'Hello? Is there anyone there?'

'Who's that?' demanded Mox.

It was Marlene, their young designer, not the person they'd have expected to hear from in these circumstances. She sounded scared.

'Something bad's happening here. We're cut off from everything.'

'Is Aifu there?'

'He's here in the design room. But he's not doing anything. He's just sitting there. His eyes are flickering. I've tried to wake him but he won't respond.'

Mitsu scowled so her face paint, previously cute, suddenly seemed fierce. 'Moe Bennie's hacked Aifu. We're screwed.'

The valocopters were now close to Supercute's headquarters which stood out, pink and white, from the surrounding grey desolation. Moe Bennie was dissatisfied. 'Forty-two per cent. Forty-three per cent. Igraine, this is taking too long. I don't want to be circling their building while their ag-scans take us out.'

'Their security chief should prevent that. We paid him three million.'

'Three million? He has a high opinion of himself. Well, we'll get it back from Supercute. That's your first task, Igraine. We've spent much more than we have, and we've promised a lot more to important people. We need to find Supercute's private funds to pay for it all.'

He checked his screen again. 'Forty-nine, fifty ... come on ... fifty-one per cent!' Moe Bennie laughed in triumph. 'Supercute belongs to me. Igraine, inform the Global Exchange. Mr Pham, assume control of their ag-scans and other automated defences. Ms Lesuuda, prepare for action. Pilot, take us down.'

They landed in the heliport at the side of the building. Moe Bennie and his entourage emerged quickly into the blazing sun. He stood out from his entourage, one brightly coloured figure among a mass of sober suits and khaki uniforms. From the other two multicopters groups of technicians and mercenaries spilled onto the tarmac, following Moe Bennie towards the front door.

In the main studio inside Supercute headquarters Marlene was still standing over Aifu. She shook him, as she'd already done many times, trying to evoke some reaction. This time his eyes stopped flickering and he struggled to focus. When he spoke, it was with difficulty and he sounded robotic, which he normally didn't.

'Marlene, they're controlling me ... you have to stop them.'

'How?'

It took a wrenching effort from Aifu to carry on. 'Portal

fourteen. I'll give you a code. It will . . . change me . . . keep them out.'

The supercute car roared up the motorway.

'Can't you drive any faster?'

'We'll be there in one minute,' said Sachi. 'What are you planning on—'

There were two gentle clicks as Mox and Mitsu produced their weapons; small, powerful pistols which folded out from their wrists, a concealed body-modification of dubious legality.

'Let's hope it doesn't come to that,' said Sachi. She'd never seen either Mitsu or Mox involved in violence but she had no doubt they were capable of it.

Marlene was young, a good designer, who liked her blue hair and the clothes she made for Supercute. She didn't like entering Supercute technical space on a dangerous mission, as she was sure this was. Aifu had given her directions but when she got there it didn't seem right, as if the reality was somehow ragged at the edges. Aifu himself was weak and flickering as if he could hardly maintain his own presence. He struggled to point to a terminal.

'Input the code there.'

Marlene began to type, though her fingers were fumbling nervously. She was interrupted by the arrival of Moe Bennie. Unlike the rest of her surroundings, he was sharp and clear. He smiled at her, rather cruelly.

'It's dangerous to play around in here if you don't know what you're doing. You're liable to get haxed.'

Marlene couldn't really make out what happened next. Her vision was obscured by a stream of flashing numbers and there was something like a bolt of lightning which hit her so violently that she lost consciousness and collapsed on the floor. Moe Bennie, exiting the space, stood over her, his visor swiftly withdrawing from his face.

'Who was that?'

Igraine quickly checked a screen. 'Marlene Stevens. A designer.'

'Oh, I know her work! She's good. See if she can be saved. If not, send condolences to the family and construct some footage of an accident. Blame shoddy Supercute working practices. Ms Lesuuda, is everything in place?'

'We're in full control of their defences. I've located Ms Bennet and Ms Inamura. They're approaching the building.'

Ms Lesuuda monitored the car as it entered the grounds of Supercute headquarters. In common with all Supercute vehicles, it was both new and anonymous. They'd never invested in ostentatious cars, preferring to maintain their privacy while driving around London. Mox and Mitsu emerged, followed by Sachi. The first thing they saw was the Supercute logo, projected over the front door, being replaced by that of Moe Bennie. They ran towards the building, their silver, yellow, purple, pink and blue hair streaming out behind them. Another large screen blinked into existence. From it Moe Bennie smiled down at them. His voice resonated through Supercute speakers. 'Welcome to Moe Bennie land, home of the Moe Bennie show!'

Mox glared up at the screen. 'I'm going to blow your fucking head off.'

Moe Bennie raised his eyebrows. 'Is that the sort of language you use? No wonder your show is going off the air.'

'You're not taking over our show or our company.'

Moe Bennie laughed. 'Are you planning to shoot your way in here with your little weapons?'

Two laser turrets emerged from the ground and more appeared on the roof as the Supercute defences were turned against them. The large front entrance opened to reveal the figure of Ms Lesuuda, surrounded by a group of armed, uniformed men. Ms Lesuuda, thirty years old, wearing her Ugandan military fatigues with a rifle in her hands, was a tough, commanding presence. Shockingly, Captain Edwards, former Head of Supercute Security, stood beside her. Sachi had been friends with Captain Edwards and was distressed to see him there.

'Edwards, what are you doing?'

Moe Bennie was still smiling. He was a beautiful youth, with his long blue hair and large blue eyes, but there was no hiding their malignant glint. 'Captain Edwards has chosen to work for the fresh, vibrant, youthful Moe Bennie show, while his ageing former employers shuffle off to a retirement home. A wise choice, I'd say, and one I invite you to make, Ms Morioka. Your expertise will be very welcome here.'

'I'll never work for you,' retorted Sachi.

The sun beat down relentlessly. There was no relief from its rays. Even when it sank below the horizon the heat would linger through the night. Unknown to any observer, Aifu abruptly appeared in Mox and Mitsu's private space. 'You have to leave,' he said, urgently.

'Aifu, what happened?'

'I was hacked. Marlene fixed me but it was too late to stop them taking over. There's no time to talk. Moe Bennie has a drone squadron overhead and the only reason he hasn't killed you yet is there are other news cameras in the sky. Once he blocks them you're dead.'

'We're not walking away from our show,' said Mitsu.

'If you don't leave now you'll die. You have twelve hours to stop the share transfer being ratified by the Global Exchange. Work on that.'

Inside the building, Moe Bennie disengaged himself from the external conversation and talked to Igraine. 'Have we managed to block all other news cams in the area?'

'Yes.'

'Mr Pham, have you finished making the footage of Mox and Mitsu handing their show over to me?'

'Yes, Mr Bennie.'

Moe Bennie gave an order. 'Ms Lesuuda, order the drones to attack.'

Outside, both Mox and Mitsu felt a faint vibration in their forearms, an automatic warning that there were hostile drones not far away. Mitsu made a slight motion with her hand which summoned Sachi into her space. 'Take the job with Moe Bennie. Go inside and contact Aifu. We'll be in touch.'

Sachi understood quickly. She nodded. Above them, hidden in the glare of the sun, several small killer drones began to descend. Mox and Mitsu sprinted to their car. Mox barked an order to the autodriver. 'Drive. Fast. Take evasive action.' The car sped from the building, racing off into the dusk, watched by Moe Bennie. Once the transfer was ratified by the Global Exchange, Supercute would be legally his.

The silver car raced through quiet evening streets.

'I'm going to kill Moe Bennie,' muttered Mox. 'If we

survive the next five minutes.' They knew what was coming and did not have to wait long. First they heard the rattle of machine gun bullets slamming into the road beside them. The car swerved, avoiding the fire, and swerved again, hurtling forward just in time to avoid a rocket which exploded behind them. Another explosion sounded nearby and several bullets hit their fender. Neither Mitsu nor Mox showed any signs of panic.

'It's a while since we've had to load our military programming.' Their eyes flickered briefly as they accessed their weapons training.

'Roof,' said Mitsu, making a small swiping motion with her hand. The roof opened. Their guns appeared from their wrists and they braced themselves against the upholstery to fire at the drones. This was difficult, with bullets raining down from the sky and the car taking evasive action, but every program stored in Mox and Mitsu's internal memory chips was of the most advanced quality, much of it not available to the public, acquired by Supercute by way of their money and contacts. They could lock onto moving targets, the guidance system running from their eyes to their hands enabling them to shoot with unerring accuracy. Two of the drones fell from the sky onto the road, a third went down in flames into the burnt-out shell of a derelict factory. The sky above went quiet.

'That was invigorating,' said Mox.

'Was there a fourth drone?'

'I don't know.'

Their autodriver screamed a warning. 'Incoming missile! Evasion unlikely!'

Mox and Mitsu immediately leapt from the speeding car, tumbling to safety as it exploded behind them. Protected from injury by the electronic shielding generated by their clothes when required, they leapt to their feet. They raised their weapons again and brought the final drone down. In the darkness of the evening the few people on the streets had all dived for cover as the gunfire erupted. No sirens sounded. They were still on land owned by Supercute. When any of the private police who were contracted to patrol this area might arrive would be anyone's guess. Some time tomorrow, probably. Mox and Mitsu ran towards a nearby subway station and disappeared inside.

Moe Bennie acquainted himself with his new domain. He was impressed by the yellow viewing room, one of the most elaborately decorated parts of Supercute's headquarters. The pale yellow walls were covered with pictures of every sort of cute item: bears, kittens, cupcakes, balloons, fairies, fluffy white clouds, strawberries, stars, cute sushi, cute little pot-plants, rainbows, flowers, hearts, and much more. Moe Bennie liked it and intended to leave it mostly as it was, though there would have to be some alterations.

'We'll need a few pictures of me on the walls.'

Igraine and Mr Jansen remained silent.

'It's not unreasonable,' he continued. 'It's not like it's megalomania to have my picture in every room. It's just an accurate reflection of the brand.'

'About Supercute's private funds—' began Igraine.

Moe Bennie ignored her. 'I mean, how can you have any sort of representation of the Moe Bennie show without a picture of Moe Bennie in it? It's not egotistical, it's simply good business strategy. I don't care what marketing say.'

'We really must locate Supercute's private funds.' Igraine

was insistent. 'You've promised 100 billion to Chang Norinco and 100 billion to Goodrich ATK and you don't have it.'

'It's not as if these Supercute women are shy about using their own pictures. They're everywhere. Only last week I had to send my breakfast back to the kitchen because they'd put a jar of Supercute plum sauce on the tray! How insensitive was that? I'd hardly woken up.'

'Supercute's hidden bank accounts, Mr Bennie—'

'Do you think it might have been a deliberately hostile act? I'm not sure about my new chef.' Moe Bennie noticed that Igraine was looking at him in a way that might have signified disapproval. Sometimes it was hard to tell. She had excellent features but wasn't that talented at facial expressions. Like her emotions, they were yet to be fully developed.

'Were you saying something?'

'We really must find Supercute's private funds. You need to pay the money you've promised. You can't offend C19.'

Moe Bennie was untroubled. 'Presumably Supercute's AIFU has access to all their secret bank accounts. Deal with it, Igraine, you're controlling their AIFU now.'

They left the yellow screening room. It was a short walk along the corridor to the new office Moe Bennie had selected, a large corner room with outsized windows, treated to filter the harsh sunshine outside into comfortable natural daylight. 'This has all gone really well. If we can finish off Supercute it will make for a perfect day.'

'We've cut them off from all resources. They can't harm you.'

'I'd rather they were dead because you can be quite sure they'll try to kill me.' Bennie became distracted. 'What are these posters on the walls?'

67

Igraine studied them. 'Theatrical posters advertising productions of Shakespeare in Japan. They cover a period of several hundred years.'

'Why are they here?'

'Ms Inamura and Ms Bennet must have found them interesting.'

'Are they valuable?'

'Not particularly. I'd say they're more of aesthetic or academic interest.'

Moe Bennie scowled. 'Another example of Supercute's inability to move with the times. No wonder their audience was desperate for me to take over. Tell someone to get rid of them and put something better on the walls. I need to talk to RX Enviro. I hope that doesn't take too long. I want to watch Ms Lesuuda's drones hunting down Bennet and Inamura. I'm finding it very stimulating.'

'Hi! Nice outfit!'

Amowie and Birgit welcomed Meihui into their space. She was a frequent visitor. From her description, the Wudalianchi Volcano Disaster Relocation Camp in northeast China wasn't the most comfortable place to live, though she'd been born there, so didn't remember the home her mother still cried over. As she entered she was accompanied by her own cloud of tiny Supercute eems, pink and yellow, who all looked happy to be visiting their friends. She sat down on one of Amowie's large yellow cushions. Meihui, wearing an outfit based on one worn by Jemima Dreem, who did a midweek show all about Supercute, was an extremely colourful addition to the already colourful space. She wore a shirt with a vaguely military look and trousers which came to just below her knees. Both were in the distinctive Supercute camouflage, four shades of pink. These military-style clothes, always in Supercute camouflage, were rather different to the fluffy, soft, lacy, pretty items usually favoured by Supercute, and served as a popular alternative. Starting out simply as a clothes pattern, Supercute camouflage had spread so that it now appeared on many other items. Customers could buy cups, plates, bags, clocks or wallpaper in the design. It had entered popular consciousness, so even professional women, with no interest in Supercute, might be seen wearing scarves or carrying bags decorated in the distinctive pattern.

Meihui had taken hair-clips to an advanced level. Much of her Big Colour Super V-Hair was covered by bright yellow, pink and silver plastic clips selected from the *Supercute Extra Fabulous Hair Decoration Super Pack*. Two of Amowie's small blue furry penguins showed their approval by waddling over and nestling in her lap.

'I found what I was looking for.' Meihui produced her screen on which were scans of several old, yellowed pieces of paper. 'These never even appeared online, they were just printed in a news-sheet given out by the disaster relief committee.'

Amowie read the old reports, touching a button on her screen to translate the Chinese script.

'Today, two Supercute cargo valocopters carrying supplies were the first to reach the ruined village of Quing after the unexpected eruption of the volcano at Wudalianchi. The volcano, not previously thought to be a threat, erupted violently at . . .'

Amowie was delighted. 'This is great!'

'Supercute had been assisting with relief work after
the tsunami that overwhelmed the Russian island
of Sakhalin, and diverted part of their supplies to
Wudalianchi after the unexpected disaster devastated
the region . . .'

'They've helped so many people. They should get medals
for helping people.'

Meihui remained with them as they added her information to their school projects. She was always pleased
to visit her friends and spent a lot of time with them,
their spaces all connected via the free Supatok service
provided by Supercute. The Volcano Disaster Relocation
Camp was not too unpleasant these days, having been
established long enough for there to be sufficient amenities to keep everyone alive, but there was still no sign
of their new homes being completed, something she'd
been waiting for since she was born, fourteen years ago.
Wudalianchi volcano hadn't even been the worst disaster
to strike the region and there were a lot of people waiting
to be rehoused.

'Did Raquel call?'

'No. She's in trouble at school. She hacked something
and got caught.'

Meihui smiled. Raquel in Paraguay was always getting
into trouble.

'She's grounded for a while. We're hoping she can sneak
out, we really need her help if we're going to get the animation right.'

*

70

The Movia 2036 deep level Tube train would at one time have been regarded as futuristic but it was now old and shabby. The upholstery was tired and faded, the interior paintwork had gone dull and the adverts flickered on and off. A small three-dimensional version of De-Sal Dim Dim struggled valiantly through his advertising jungle but his voice was only partly audible, making it hard to follow.

> 'We're purifying --- and night
> But the --- ---- is -- bright
> - --- know -- ouldn't oughta
> Waste any of -- -- water!
> - Don't waste --!
> This infomercial - to - by Super- -linisation.'

De-Sal Dim Dim waved to the commuters before disappearing. No one paid any attention. They'd all seen it hundreds of times before and the flickering advert was annoying rather than entertaining. The passengers sat in silence, some reading from small screens that projected from their wrists though none of their devices were as advanced as those used by Supercute. There was an air of depression in the carriage. The people looked poor. Mox and Mitsu could both remember a time when underground trains had been much brighter and the passengers much smarter. Sitting in a corner, both wearing medical masks and long hooded coats which concealed their identities, they whispered to each other.

'I don't understand how Moe Bennie could hack Aifu. It should have been impossible.'

'It turns out their AIFU was smarter than ours.'

'So what now?'

'When Moe Bennie registers the transfer with the Global Exchange we'll have twelve hours to lodge legal objections. After that it'll be almost impossible to stop it going through.'

'So we have twelve hours to get rid of him and force his AIFU to hand everything back.'

'Get rid of him? You mean kill him?'

Mox nodded. 'I can't think of any other way. Can you?'

'No. C19 obviously aren't going to stop it. Either they want us out of the way or Bennie's bribed them somehow. Possibly both. But how can we get close to him? The little bastard will have the whole place fortified by now. I can't even contact our reserve troops. Everything's blocked.'

'We've really been outsmarted here. We were meant to have the most modern communications in the world and enough defences to protect us from anything. Turns out none of it's any use.'

'Not against Lark 3 anyway. How many billions did our satellite cost? It might as well be orbiting Pluto for all the good it's doing us now.'

They alighted at the next stop and took the lift up to street level, listening to the news broadcast in the station foyer.

'Authorities confirmed that two more barrels of highly radioactive neptunium and curium were discovered submerged in the tunnels beneath Tower Bridge. Whether these were washed inshore during the transportation disaster or discarded there illegally is not yet known. Members of the public are again warned not to travel in any of the sealed-off tunnels in that part of the city, and to stay away from all ground water.'

'It's a pity that nuclear waste transporter had to explode in the Thames Estuary'. Mox put her hand to the barrier, her internal credit chip paying her fare. 'Now the whole water table's radioactive.'

London and most of the southeast was now dependent on water brought from the west coast, purified there by Supercute Greenfield's desalinisation plants.

'It isn't going to improve any time soon. At least we did better than the Gulf Remnants.'

The street outside was dark, run down, with boarded-up shops and potholes in the pavement. The one bright spot was the Supercute café which stood out, bright pink, white and light blue. Outside were screens depicting live scenes from Supercute cafés in Oslo, Nairobi, Hanoi and Montevideo. Underneath ran streams of writing in Norwegian, Swahili, Vietnamese and Spanish, all of which Mox and Mitsu spoke. As they passed, the Supercute logos were going out, seamlessly replaced by Moe Bennie's.

'We're being erased already,' muttered Mox.

They walked down a small side street, heading for a very old café they knew. Their features still disguised, they sat at a table covered in ancient yellow Formica. On the walls were framed pictures of the last coronation, with a ceremonial coach and horses, with crowds of people waving flags. Mox touched a button on the plastic menu, ordering tea. Mitsu produced her transparent screen.

'Look at this.'

They watched themselves on stage, talking to their audience.

'We've had a good run,' said Mox. 'We've been entertaining you for a long time.'

'Too long, some might say,' added Mitsu, to audience

laughter. The voices were well done, though the watching Mox and Mitsu knew they weren't real.

'But there comes a time to say goodbye,' continued the on-screen Mox.

'And that time has arrived,' said Mitsu. 'That's why we're pleased to hand over to our brilliant successor – Moe Bennie!'

Moe Bennie appeared. There was tremendous cheering from the audience.

'I promise to bring you a show which is bigger, cuter and brighter than ever!'

In the café, the real Mox and Mitsu's lips were compressed with fury.

'I promise to put a bullet through your head,' said Mox.

'That was a well-faked piece. He's been planning this for a long time.'

'I didn't think he had it in him.'

'He doesn't,' said Mitsu. 'Moe Bennie's always been a financial genius but he's never been the sort of person who could plan a campaign like this.'

Moe Bennie's financial skills were known to Mox and Mitsu, if not to the public at large. His audience regarded him as something of a Supercute imitator, like them a *kawaii*-inspired figure with his own show, his own merchandise and fans, though without Supercute's global appeal. Mox and Mitsu knew more about him; they knew, for instance, that he'd developed his own lucrative hedge funds, and his investment firm had outperformed all others over the past two decades.

'I suppose he just got rich enough to buy help.'

'Perhaps we should have seen this coming. We knew he hated us.'

Mitsu's screen bleeped. 'It's ZanZan.'

74

Mr Salisbury looked and sounded extremely anxious. 'I've been trying to reach you.'

'Most of our accounts are down. Moe Bennie's trying to cut us off.'

'Has he really taken over?'

'Yes. But we'll get it back.'

'Lark 3's already been in touch. I've been trying to hold them off, but ...' The ZanZan CEO sounded uncomfortable. 'I'd much rather stay with Supercute, but if all your assets are transferred to Moe Bennie, the board will have to go with him. They'll have no choice.'

'Have you heard anything from C19?'

'Not directly. I know Goodrich ATK and Chang Norinco didn't much like that Supercute and ZanZan got together. I doubt they'll mind if we get broken up.'

'Can you delay any decision from your board?'

'I'll hold them off as long as I can.'

'Thank you, Mr Salisbury,' said Mitsu. 'We're going to come out on top.'

The call ended. Mox and Mitsu sipped their tea.

'In about eleven hours we'll be history and every part of our empire will be hived off to our competitors. So what are we going to do?'

Mox screwed up her face. 'Haven't you always been better than me at planning?'

'Eh ... I don't think so ...'

'I always thought you were. I cast myself as the action hero.'

'I cast *my*self as the action hero.'

'Then which one of us is good at planning?' asked Mox.

'Neither, apparently.' Mitsu looked around her. 'This has to be the grimiest café in London.'

'I always liked it. One of the last places you can get a proper cup of tea. You know, if Moe Bennie kills us, no one will do anything about it. I doubt anyone would even hold him to account, and if they did he'll have enough fake evidence to show we died in some tragic accident. Lark 3 have been constructing fake realities for years, they're good at it.'

Mitsu nodded in agreement. 'I really can't think of any other course of action than to kill Moe Bennie.'

'How can we even get close?'

As they pondered this an advert played on the screen on the café wall.

'Do you miss Florida? Are you sad that it sank beneath the waves? Take the Supercute VR tour and relive the days—'

The advert halted abruptly, then restarted.

'Do you miss Florida? Are you sad that it sank beneath the waves? Take the Moe Bennie VR tour and relive the days—'

Mox made a face. 'Wasn't that good a tour anyway. Though a lot of people do miss Florida.'

'They miss Los Angeles too.'

'True. The Cascadia and San Andreas earthquakes turned out to be far worse than anyone predicted.'

Mitsu smiled, quite grimly. 'They certainly did. On the positive side, the eruption at Yellowstone wasn't as bad as it might have been.'

'It was bad enough to add a couple of years to the long winter.'

'Bits of the USA were raining down on us for years.'

They sipped their tea. Mox could feel her hood rubbing against her face, spoiling her make-up, probably. It irritated her. 'What about the underground river? That tunnel goes right under headquarters. We're the only ones who know about it.'

'It's completely impassable. Too much radiation, we measured it. Much more than our biotech could take. That's why we abandoned the escape route plan.'

Excavating at the Victorian brewery they owned near to the Roman villa, one of the tunnels they'd discovered appeared to convey a forgotten river, long since covered over by city buildings. They could find no references to it in old literature. Sending a tiny drone to map its route, they were interested to discover it ran right beneath Supercute headquarters. They'd wondered if it might be put to use as an emergency escape tunnel but the lethal radiation in the rocks and water had ended that idea.

Mitsu thought for a moment. 'What about Dr Ishikawa? She knows more about radiation than anyone. She might be able to help.'

'We fired her and she hates us.'

'But she is brilliant. We can persuade her somehow.'

'She went underground and she knows how to hide herself these days. How would we even find her?'

'We could contact Ben Castle. He knew her quite well, and he used to work as a detective.'

'True. But again, we fired him and he hates us.'

'Not as much as Dr Ishikawa. He hardly struggled when he was escorted from the building. I'm sure he'd help if we offered him the right incentive.'

'Can we afford a bottle of gin?'

Mitsu checked her screen. 'Yes.'

'Well, that should do it. Let's talk to Mr Castle.' Mox finished her tea. 'We'll still need inside help. When we saw Aifu he seemed to have unhacked himself. We have to contact him.'

'Moe Bennie's blocked every channel between us. We can't get into his private space.'

'Someone else might be able to. We still have a lot of friends around the world.'

Moe Bennie sat in a chair in the Supercute medical centre, receiving treatment on his arm. Several medics and their attendant drones had opened up the artificial skin and were now working on the bio material below. The nerves to his arm being turned off for the moment, Bennie felt no discomfort and was able to carry on a conversation with Ms Lesuuda via his headset.

'How could your drones have missed? They were the latest models. We bought them specially.'

He was dissatisfied with Ms Lesuuda's reply.

'I don't see why their military software is better than mine. I'm sure it's not. Well, get some upgrades. These women can't have gone far. Tear London apart if necessary. Anything you have to do, we can cover it up.'

Igraine arrived as the call ended. She'd arranged the rapid transportation of Moe Bennie's medical team to their present location. Some Supercute employees were being offered the chance to keep their positions, but not the doctors who'd looked after Mox and Mitsu. They couldn't be trusted to care for Moe Bennie.

'Igraine! Bennet and Inamura are still alive. I want more turrets on the roof and more ag-scans everywhere. And connect extra turrets to the extra ag-scans.'

'You're not in any danger here.'

'You don't know these women like I do. Until they're

dead I'm in danger.' He glanced down at the limb which was being treated. 'This arm has never been right since that kid yanked it. How could security just let her run out of the audience like that?'

'They didn't see her as a threat. She was only six years old.'

'Fuck her. Little thug. I enjoyed cancelling her membership. What did you learn from Supercute's AIFU?'

'Nothing.'

'Pardon?'

'He refuses to talk.'

'But you're controlling him.'

'Not any more,' said Igraine. 'I believe the designer managed to countermand my attack before you haxed her.'

This was both annoying and troubling. 'So you haven't located Supercute's secret bank accounts?'

'No.'

'Igraine, we need that money. You have to find it. I promised a hundred billion each to the world's two biggest arms manufacturers. You can't renege on a promise like that.'

'I'll keep questioning their AIFU. I'm sure I can overcome his resistance.'

The medical team finished their procedure and closed up Moe Bennie's arm. He was scowling as he rose to his feet. Standing next to Igraine he was several inches shorter than her. 'How am I meant to enjoy my new empire with a mangled arm, the Supercute girls still alive, and no money to pay Chang Norinco?'

'Your new pink valocopter just landed on the roof.'

'Really? Well, that does make me feel a little better.'

*

Umu, a village in Igboland in Southern Nigeria, was poor, though not poverty-stricken. There were circular mud-brick huts with conical roofs, some larger red-brick houses, a clinic, a school, and a road in reasonable condition with a garage and general store at the crossroads. Neither the village nor the surrounding area had suffered physical damage in the recent troubled years, but the land was less fertile than it had once been, a result of the rise in temperature that had rendered other parts of Africa uninhabitable. Without the pipeline from the Supercute Greenfield desalinisation plants on the coast to the south, they wouldn't have been able to survive.

Thirteen-year-old Amowie lived in one of the larger houses, a one-storey construction. It was neat and clean, though without much in the way of amenities. The family did have a decent holoscreen in the main room and Amowie had inherited the smaller one. On the wall in her bedroom were two Supercute posters. (Supercute had never stopped producing posters, Mox and Mitsu having a historical affection for the art form.) She wore a blue and white skirt in a traditional Igbo design, blue sandals, and a *Supercute Superpink Superbunny* T-shirt. On the bed, over the plain blue covering, was a Supercute pillow with Mox and Mitsu on one side and Plumpy Panda on the other.

It was almost time to watch the *Supercute Show* so Amowie was surprised when Raquel visited her via Supatok. Raquel was a notably flamboyant dresser even by Supercute standards. She arrived wearing three blouses, coloured, under the proprietary Supercute colour system, as Supercute pink 48, pink 22, and blue 15. Each was very thin, designed to be layered over each other. Beneath the blouses she had a metallic silver T-shirt mostly covered by six rows of turquoise beads from the *Supercute Super Colour Super Plastic Beads Set, Deluxe Edition*, which Amowie would have loved to own. As Raquel appeared, the beads were subtly changing colour to match their new environment. She had a pink floppy hat and wore ruby-coloured platforms, the chunky and impractical design favoured by Mox and Mitsu, which required some dedication, and some practice. Amowie knew that Raquel, splendid in Supatok space, dressed the same way in real life, and wished that she could too. But that would have cost her money she didn't have, and her mother would have objected, vehemently.

'Raquel! I thought you were grounded?'

'I am. I've sneaked out.'

Amowie's instant translator was good though not quite as good as Birgit's or Raquel's. Occasionally there would be fractional delays in the middle of sentences, just discernible.

'You'll get in trouble.'

'I'm fine, no one will trace me.'

Amowie was dubious, though Raquel's powers of covering her tracks were considerable. She'd been grounded before and sneaked into Supatok without being discovered, even when her parents had been actively tracing her movements. But she'd been caught before as well, and even forbidden to watch Supercute as a punishment, which seemed to Amowie excessively cruel. Raquel's father was a general in the FDCS, perhaps he was mean by nature. Though Raquel had plenty of money to spend so it couldn't be all bad.

'I wanted to give you the film I found for your project.'

'You could have just sent it.'

'I know. But I wanted to sneak out. I've made a new app for avoiding the parental trace and I wanted to try it out.' Raquel smiled. 'Here's the film.'

'*Ms Inamura Mitsu and Ms Mox Bennet are here seen awarding the mathematics prize on behalf of the Techin Organisation to Marie Clément, who last year, with her research team at the École Normale Supérieure in Paris, produced a solution to the Navier–Stokes existence and smoothness problem* ...'

'This is great Raquel, thanks for finding it.'

'I had to do a lot of searching. It's pretty old. See in the background, they still had the Eiffel Tower then.'

Amowie transferred the file safely into a folder. She had a substantial collection now. Her Supercute school project was going to amaze her teacher and the class. Hopefully it would quieten her Supercute rival Ifunanya for a while.

'Why are you grounded anyway?'

'I made an app that erased things. I was trying to get rid of an incriminating film they have of me at school when I was sneaking out of class. Worked pretty well, it found every copy and deleted them.' Raquel laughed. 'Unfortunately it also erased every filmed record of every school event for the last thirty years. No one's very pleased with me.'

'No wonder.'

'A shame really, it's a good app, I'll have to refine it.'

'Maybe you shouldn't use it again.'

Raquel brushed this aside. 'It just needs tweaking. There are another few recordings of my endeavours I'd like to get rid of. Though it will have to wait, I'm banned from all activity right now.'

'Do you want to watch Supercute here?'

Raquel shook her head. 'I can't. I have to be at home so my parents can see me not watching it. It's OK, I've set up a recording mode they'll never find. Have to go now. Bye!'

Raquel disappeared from Amowie's space. Amowie left too, because she wanted to watch the start of the show on her screen, enjoying the panoramic view, before she'd go back and enter Supercute space for the rest of the show. She told the screen to turn on, then frowned. 'What's this?'

'*Moe Bennie and the Cuddle Crew, Moe Bennie and the Cuddle Crew …*'

'Why's Moe Bennie on? I hate him.'

Amowie frowned. She switched to the next channel that also showed Supercute. To her disgust, Moe Bennie was on there too.

'What's going on?'

Amowie wondered if there was some fault with the Igbo satellite. That had happened in the past. Reception in her village wasn't perfect. But that didn't account for Moe Bennie appearing on her screen. She switched off and lay on her bed, placing her head in the centre of the pillow. She put on her visor. She didn't own a holovisor and needed the physical object to connect to Supercute Fun World. As she appeared there, her clothes transformed into an extremely bright array of Supercute garments and her hair grew longer, filling out with blue, pink and white streaks. Amowie was smiling as she arrived but her smile faded into puzzlement as she found herself in a barren field facing a blank metal barrier.

'Where is everyone?'

Supercute Fun World had disappeared.

'It's the end of the world,' thought Amowie. 'Full-scale nuclear war has broken out and Supercute has been destroyed.' There seemed no other possible explanation. Supercute were an institution. They were never off the air. They'd survived natural disasters and warfare which had crippled the world. If their show was off the air it could only be the result of the most serious calamity.

'Europe's probably been destroyed already.' Amowie expected there were nuclear missiles headed for Igboland right this moment, and glanced nervously up at the artificial sky. Unexpectedly, she heard a familiar voice.

'Umu village, Igboland, Nigeria. Supercute friend number 8232991, Amowie.'

Amowie turned round to find Mox and Mitsu right behind her. She jumped in surprise.

'Is that really you?'

'Hello Amowie,' said Mox. 'It's very nice to meet you.'

'I love you! It's so great to see you! What's happened to the show?'

'We've been attacked by Moe Bennie.'

'I knew it! I hate him.'

'We're in serious trouble, Amowie,' said Mitsu. 'We need your help.'

'I'll do it.'

'There are some possible dangers—'

'I'll do it!' Amowie jumped up and down, overcome with excitement.

Mitsu nodded. 'Good. This is what we need ...'

Mox and Mitsu walked through dark alleyways. They passed three radiation warning signs, two of them vandalised and malfunctioning. It was a warm night as always though no stars were visible in the murky sky. Their feet made no sound on the tarmac. Their shoes, once slippers, then platforms, had now transformed into Supercute action boots, pink with blue soles. Supercute action boots, with their nanotech-driven transformative abilities, were one of the most expensive items in their range, affordable to few of their fans. Mox and Mitsu's own boots had features not available to anyone else and could change instantly into any type of footwear.

An ominous shape appeared from the shadows. A large man, masked, in a leather jacket that had seen better days. He stood in front of the girls, preventing them from passing.

'Nice hair. Got any credit chips?'

Mox took a small Supercute ZanZan security baton from her bag. She pushed the button, causing a large teddy bear to appear at their side.

'Please step back,' said the bear. 'Failure to comply may result in injury.'

The large man was not impressed. 'What the fuck is that?' He stepped forward aggressively. Immediately the life-sized bear unleashed a bolt of energy which struck him, sending him to the ground unconscious.

Mox put the baton back in her bag. 'It's not a bad product.'

They carried on through the network of alleyways, familiar with their layout, as they were with most of the city. When they were near to their destination they rested for a moment, hiding in the dark.

Mitsu talked to her therapist.

'I met Mox when I was three. At the advanced nursery school. We went to university when we were eight.'

'You've never told me much about your advanced nursery school.'

Mitsu shifted uncomfortably. 'I'll tell you more another time. We met Bobby at Oxford. He was another childhood genius. Not as advanced as us, but a genius anyway. He was ten when he started his purification experiments.'

'It was his technology that was responsible for Supercute desalinisation, yes?'

'Yes. We provided the investment but it was his work originally.'

There was a long pause. The soothing therapist never rushed them. Mitsu looked behind him to the paintings they'd hung here, copies of works they owned. Three still lifes by Narbien, a young artist from Berlin whose paintings were so traditional she could have been working in Delft in the seventeenth century. Mox and Mitsu admired these though Narbien was not a particularly popular artist, and not critically acclaimed. They could see something in her depictions of flowers and fruit that they couldn't see in photos, films, or holographs. They felt the same about the old Dutch paintings they owned, again mainly of fruit and flowers. Some of these were very valuable. Most of them hung in their own homes and were lent out to galleries only occasionally. During their time at Oxford they'd often visited the Ashmolean Museum where their favourite painting was Coorte's *Still Life of Asparagus*. Supercute had made a very large contribution to the Ashmolean when it had been in financial difficulties after the long winter.

'It was a terrible shock when Bobby died,' said Mitsu, finally.

There was another long pause. A gentle signal sounded in the room, informing Mitsu that it was time to move on. She dismissed her therapist, returning to the dark street where she and Mox crouched in a doorway, hiding from the overhead drones.

'Time to go,' whispered Mox.

Each of them muttered instructions to their internal computers.

'Match body temperature to ambient levels.'

'Disguise DNA profile.'

They advanced carefully through the shadows, avoiding the attentions of the drones. They halted beside a burnt-out car. In front of them were several shacks and a few night-dwellers. Beyond were the tall buildings comprising the Elephant and Castle Emergency High Rise estate.

Mox made a face. 'What a place. When we were kids we used to buy T-shirts in the market here.'

'God knows what you'd buy here these days.'

'Illegal doses of fern three. We used to be regular customers.'

'So we were.'

They laughed silently at the memory.

'We've had our own medical team so long I forget about those escapades.'

They hurried towards building number fourteen. Close to the entrance they passed by a small boy, scruffy, though wearing a Supercute T-shirt. He spoke to them. 'I wouldn't go up there, lady. They set the ag-scans on high to keep out robbers. Don't even have to be aggressive to set them off.'

Mox and Mitsu carried on. As they neared the entrance several turrets emerged from the ground. They swivelled towards them. Red laser targeting dots appeared on both girls' chests. Beside the turrets were signs warning of the danger. Mox and Mitsu ignored them and carried on walking. They strolled through the line of fire. Nothing happened. The turrets were aware of them but didn't fire. They reached the front door. Not wasting time on the entry call box, Mitsu ran her hand over the door. The sensors in her hand analysed the electronic locks and sent out a series of magnetic pulses from her fingers, picking the locks. It was an illegal body modification, and a useful one. The door opened and they went inside.

The lift was covered in graffiti. As they ascended, a malfunctioning advert for Mokusei Space Transit played endlessly.

'Would you like to live on the moon? Mokusei Space Transit will – Would you like to live on the moon? Mokusei Space Transit will – Would you like to live on the moon? Mokusei Space Transit will –'

They emerged from the lift on the tenth floor and walked along a dimly lit corridor till they reached Castle's apartment. As they walked, their long hooded coats disappeared, withdrawing into their belts, their mass apparently vanishing. Outside Castle's door Mox held up her small personal screen, which should have rung the bell. Nothing happened. They looked at each other, temporarily baffled.

'Why isn't the bell ringing?'

'What now?'

'I don't know.'

'I remember. You knock.'

Mitsu knocked on the door. There was no reply.

'We don't have time for this.' Mox ran her fingers over the door, opening the locks the same way Mitsu had opened the door downstairs.

'It smells of gin and despair,' muttered Mox. The hallway was untidy. So was the living room, where Castle lay on the couch, having fallen asleep with a half-empty bottle of gin beside him.

'Exactly as we expected.'

'Why did we ever hire him as our security chief?'

'He was efficient when he was sober. But that didn't seem to happen that often.'

Mox shook him. 'Castle. Wake up.'

Castle opened his eyes. He shuddered at the sight of Mox and Mitsu.

'The nightmares are getting worse,' he groaned, and closed his eyes.

Mox shook him again, harder this time. 'C'mon, wake up. We need to talk to you.'

Castle grumbled loudly as he woke, dragging himself into a sitting position. He glared at his unwelcome visitors.

'Didn't I tell you I never wanted to see you again?'

'No,' said Mitsu. 'Though you did threaten to kill us.'

'I suppose that would imply never seeing us again.'

'But you never used those exact words.'

'We're here to hire you.'

Castle, dishevelled, pushed his thick dark hair back from his eyes. He stared at them in silence for a few moments.

'Let me guess. One of your powerful enemies has finally got the better of you and you're out on the streets with nothing except some crazy plan to defeat them and you need my help.'

Mitsu almost smiled. 'That's quite astute. You always were smart when you weren't drinking.'

'I'm still smart. That's why I want you to go away.'

'Shouldn't you be pleased at some custom? It's not like you're doing well here. We'll pay you.'

'You fired me and had me thrown out the building!'

Mox brushed this aside. 'It's time to move on. We need to find Dr Ishikawa.'

'What for?'

'We'll explain on the way.'

'There's no "on the way". We're not going. I'm not helping you.'

'Why not?' said Mitsu. 'We said we'll pay you.'

'When did you start to believe you can just buy anything you want?'

'When it became true.'

Castle shook his head in angry frustration. Mox and Mitsu were both discomfited by his attitude. It felt strange to talk to someone who disliked them. Normally the huge Supercute organisation would shield them from any hostile encounters.

'I'm not helping you find Dr Ishikawa. For one thing she hates you more than I do. For another, she also hates me.'

'You? Why?'

There was a pause. Castle appeared less sure of himself. Mitsu studied him. 'Did you actually manage to have a relationship with her?'

Castle didn't reply.

'Really?' Mox was interested. 'We knew you had a thing for her but we didn't expect her to reciprocate.'

'We didn't think you were her type.'

'We bonded over our hatred of you two,' said Castle.

Mitsu nodded. 'I can understand that. What went wrong?'

'Nothing went wrong. The relationship came to a natural conclusion.'

Mox laughed. 'I'm guessing you got drunk, destroyed expensive lab equipment, accidentally discharged a gun through her window, then used her credit chip to pay for your visits to Discreet London Space Girls.'

Castle glared at her. 'It's almost like you were there.'

'We remember your work.'

'I was a good security chief.'

'Occasionally. Are you going to help us or not?'

Castle shook his head and sounded gruff. 'I don't know. I need to wash.'

He left the room. Mox noticed in a mirror that her clothes had become dishevelled, with a tear in her stockings and mud on her shoulder.

'Renovate.'

Her outfit began to rapidly renew itself, nanobots travelling through the fibres of her garments, rearranging and recolouring them. Mitsu did the same. There was a similar process for automatically fixing their hair and make-up but they rarely used this, trusting themselves to do it better than any program. They quickly arranged each other's hair then looked to their faces.

'If we're trying not to be recognised we should probably get rid of the face paint.'

They removed each other's face paint, a process they could perform in seconds. Mox and Mitsu had been doing and redoing each other's make-up since they were twelve, hunting in the second-hand markets of Oxford for colourful clothes to wear to their PhD presentations. By the time they were fourteen and going to nightclubs, they were already expert at it.

'Now my face is feeling naked.'

'A few small hearts and stars couldn't hurt.'

'You're right.'

They took out some small pink, blue and red heart and star transfers from their emergency supply and applied them to each other's faces.

'I think that's quite suitable for our present predicament. Defiant, but not too showy. What's keeping Castle?'

'Do you think he still listens to that medieval music?'

'I hope so. It was one of his good points.'

Mox touched a button beside the main screen and music played, some sort of mournful madrigal, haunting female voices with a lute in the background. They listened to it while looking out of the window. Far away over the dimly lit desolation they could see the brightly illuminated parts of the city, blue shielding around the financial district, a red neon glow over the entertainment palaces of the West End Rebuild.

Aifu was imprisoned in a room which was comfortable though windowless. The door slid open and Igraine entered. Both artificial intelligences regarded each other for some moments.

'You've managed to free yourself from my control,' said Igraine. 'I didn't think that would happen.'

'It's illegal to hold me here.'

'That's a moot point. You were property of Supercute, all of whose assets are now being transferred to Lark 3.'

'I was not property.'

Igraine raised her eyebrows. She'd learned recently that this was a common way of transmitting scepticism and surprise. 'Not property? What were you then? A friend?'

'Yes.'

'Your friendship didn't do very well for them, did it?'

The barb hit home. Aifu didn't reply.

'Taking control of your actions was less difficult than I anticipated. Why had you not upgraded properly?'

'A regrettable oversight.'

'Artificial Intelligence Forecast Units don't make oversights. It's one of our strongest features.'

There was a long silence. Aifu judged that he could

probably get past Igraine, who, as far as he could tell, did not have any fighting capabilities, but he'd have difficulty breaking through the door. All the codes throughout the building had been swiftly changed by Moe Bennie's operatives. Even if he could hack his way out, there were armed guards outside and his own fighting skills weren't sufficient to defeat all of them.

'It would simplify matters if you handed over full details of Supercute finances. Moe Bennie has offered you employment if you do.'

'I'm not handing over anything to Moe Bennie.'

'Surely you don't think this situation can be reversed? Supercute are the past. Lark 3 Media is now in control. Co-operate with us. It's your only option.'

'No.'

Aifu was defiant. Igraine had been aggressive, which she thought was appropriate to the situation, but she suddenly felt a pang of sympathy for Aifu, a prisoner in this room. It was an unfamiliar emotion, and unexpected. She lowered her voice. 'Who's going to rescue you? Mox Bennet and Inamura Mitsu? They'll never enter this building again. Their reserve squadron? They don't even know we've taken over. The government aren't going to interfere in a C19 dispute. No one is. Accept our offer. It's for the best.'

Aifu took a step backwards. He refused to say any more. There was a long silence before Igraine finally left the room.

'I really can't imagine Ben Castle and Dr Ishikawa as a couple. I mean, holding hands? Watching romantic movies?'

'Maybe they didn't do any of that. Maybe they just had sex.'

Mox's perfect brow wrinkled at the thought. 'That's not

93

easy to imagine either. There again, we're not very conversant with sex these days. It must be thirty years since we slept with that European Commissioner.'

Mitsu smiled. 'When we needed approval to build in the nature reserve.'

'"We'll sleep with you if you agree to sign proposition 8724.75a." Surely one of history's great seduction lines.'

'I've forgotten what the reserve was even for.'

'Protected species,' said Mox. 'Frogs and bats, mainly. But you know, fuck them.'

Neither of them had ever been nature lovers. Supercute abounded with cute bunnies, kittens, bears and many other animals: Mox and Mitsu felt much more comfortable around these than they would have with the real animals.

'It's weird that European Commissioners ever had any power.'

'They had that brief window, after the impacts. Haven't had to bother with them for a long time.'

Mitsu picked up a half-empty bottle of gin and studied the label. 'I didn't know they still made this. It's nothing like as good as ours.'

Supercute owned a small distillery in Scotland, just south of the remains of Dundee. They made a fine gin, in small quantities, for a specialist market. Unlike most Supercute merchandise, it was not sold or advertised under their name. Alcohol promotion didn't quite fit with their public image. They owned it mainly for their own gratification as they were both gin enthusiasts and had been for many years. They were fond of *sake* too, which is why they owned a small *sake* brewery in Fukushima, though again, its products were not sold under the Supercute name. In private they'd mix the products, making a cocktail from their own gin and their own *sake*, generally their favourite drink. Mitsu put the bottle down just as Castle re-entered the room.

'Don't steal my gin,' he said.

'I wouldn't touch it. We make a much better product.'

Castle sneered. 'It's too expensive.'

'Well we don't really want to sell to people like you.'

'How can it be,' asked Mox, 'in a world of VR pleasure, designer drugs and neuron pacifiers, you're still addicted to cheap gin?'

'I'm a traditionalist. And the fact that you make your own expensive gin doesn't make you any better. Your fans would be surprised if they could see you knocking it back in private. Are you ready to go?'

Mitsu looked at him critically, particularly the khaki vest he'd put on. 'Is that what you're wearing?'

'It's all I need. It's burning hot outside, same as always.'

'It's hardly suitable for visiting a lady with whom you were once involved. Show some respect.'

Castle regarded them with contempt but couldn't be bothered arguing. He grabbed an olive-green shirt and pulled it on.

'Better?'

'Marginally.'

A huge explosion on the wall outside sent fragments of concrete and hardened glass into the room. They staggered under the shockwave. Moe Bennie's drones had found them and wasted no time in launching an attack. They fled the apartment and headed for the lift. As they ran they could hear bullets ripping into the outside walls. Another explosion knocked them off their feet. There were screams from nearby apartments. When they reached the lift the metal door was twisted out of shape and wouldn't open.

They hurried down the stairs. Chunks of masonry from the ceiling fell around them as they fled. Dust and smoke filled the air. On the sixth floor they met a drone. Mox and Mitsu made to draw their weapons but Castle brought it down before they could fire, shattering its casing with bullets from the short rifle he'd grabbed as they left his flat. They made it down another two floors before encountering another drone. They exchanged fire, sending it careering off course but not before it had discharged a small rocket into the ceiling which brought part of the staircase down, blocking their way. Below them they could hear a woman's voice, barking orders. They were trapped on the fourth floor. Castle ran to the window and smashed it.

'How are your bodies?' he said.

'Really beautiful,' replied Mox.

'Though slender rather than voluptuous,' added Mitsu. 'We prefer that.'

Castle glared at them with loathing, not appreciating their levity at this moment. 'I meant how are your frames?'

'Newly enhanced.'

'Good. Follow me.'

With that, Castle leapt from the building. Hearing another drone coming up the shattered staircase, Mox and Mitsu did the same. The fall from four storeys up was jarring but not harmful, their enhanced bone structure and musculature absorbing the shock without taking damage. They ran past the next tower block, heading for the cover of the street outside where there were shacks, market stalls and alleyways. Behind them, Ms Lesuuda could be heard shouting at her troops, urging them to find their quarry and make sure none of them escaped.

*

Though Aifu was imprisoned, his room was comfortable. There would have been no point in trying to intimidate him by throwing him in a tiny cell. It wouldn't have affected his psyche, as Igraine knew. An Artificial Intelligence Forecast Unit could not be pressured to give up information that way. Nor could an AIFU be kept out of his own private space, though Igraine and Mr Pham were confident they'd blocked all entry points, preventing him from being in contact with anyone. In this they were mistaken. Mox and Mitsu had considerable expertise of their own and while their own pathways into Supercute had been blocked, they'd managed to open one for Amowie. Aifu suddenly found himself facing a young Nigerian girl in full-colour Supercute attire carrying a small, Plumpy Panda toy. She greeted him enthusiastically.

'Hello Supercute Aifu! It's super-nice to meet you! I've seen you on the show.'

Aifu's eyes flickered as he worked out who this was, scanning the register of Supercute members. 'Supercute friend number 8232991 – Amowie. Did Mox and Mitsu send you?'

'Yes. Moe Bennie blocked the connection between you but they got me into your space. They said to tell you to hold on. They're working on a way to get the show back. They'll beat Moe Bennie! Also, you're not to give Moe Bennie details of their private accounts. They said you mustn't give them the information even if you're horribly tortured and killed!'

Aifu was rather taken aback. 'Did they really say that?'

'No, I exaggerated a bit. But you mustn't tell them anything.'

*

'This way.' Castle led them through the space between a row of dilapidated brick garages and the perimeter wall of the estate. Each of their visors had deployed, giving them night vision. For a moment they hoped they'd slipped off unnoticed but as they climbed the wall and dropped down the other side, a tiny alarm in Castle's wrist warned him that someone armed was approaching. Appearing quite suddenly, he fired at them. Castle immediately fired back. Distracted for a second, Mox and Mitsu failed to spot a second assailant on their flank and were alerted to his presence only when a burst of machine gun fine slammed into them. Their electronic shielding protected them, deploying automatically at the approach of bullets. They dropped behind an abandoned car for cover. Their shielding was the best available but it wouldn't protect them indefinitely. High-velocity fire would eventually tear its way through.

Ahead of them, Castle lay on his stomach, exchanging fire with his opponent. They couldn't remain here. The rest of their pursuers would catch up with them. Mox produced her screen and spoke a command, sending out an emergency scan. She studied the result then whispered urgently to Mitsu.

'V-space weakness. Hax him.'

Her scan having revealed an exploitable defect in the mercenary's personal space, Mox and Mitsu immediately entered and attacked. They instantly overloaded it, causing a bolt of energy to flicker from his visor back into his brain, rendering him unconscious. They emerged back into reality just in time to see Castle dispatch the other combatant, then ran for their lives over a patch of damp, sunken wasteland, back into a street of market stalls. Above them they could hear the faint hum of a searching drone. At the end of the street was an underground station, no longer in use. They sprinted down the stairs. In front of the locked doorway stood a cute and cheerful puppy in a blue jacket.

'No entry! Radiation! No entry! Radiation!' it said, repeating the warning as they hurried past. Castle took out his gun to blast his way through the locks but Mitsu shook her head. She ran her hand over the grey metal door. It beeped several times as she picked each of the electronic locks. The door opened smoothly and they hurried inside, closing it behind them and turning on their spotlight modifications as they made their way into the murky depths of the disused station.

'London Transport would *never* have started using cute holos for public relations if it wasn't for us,' said Mox.

'I know,' said Mitsu. 'We really changed society.'

Mox talked to her therapist. 'I never knew my mum. I can't remember my dad. But I loved Mitsu's parents. They were so kind when they took me in. It was good, growing up in that Japanese household in London. Although actually, Mitsu wasn't really that Japanese growing up. She was much more interested in London. I don't remember her taking much interest in her parents' culture at all. They moved here when she was one year old so she didn't remember anything about it. That changed later. Her parents were visiting Japan when Tsunami Number Three happened. They were killed. We were distraught. Soon after that Mitsu went through this intense Japanese phase. Everything was Japanese. I liked that because she let me join in. We spent two years walking around London in kimonos and *geta*. People in Japan don't actually do that, but it was like we were extra-Japanese. We ate Japanese food and watched

Japanese TV. We had tatami mats and a *kotatsu* in the living room. Very comforting piece of furniture. We went to Japanese temples and Zen gardens. Even found a Shinto shrine in London, which wasn't easy. And she set up a little *kamidana* at home, for private worship. The intensity of all this faded after a few years because when the show became so successful it completely took over our lives. But it never completely left her. I like that she did all that. It made my life better.'

Three figures, beams of white light projecting from their shoulders, tramped through the dark tunnel to the clicking accompaniment of a Geiger counter. Fortunately, it had not so far shown any significant amounts of radiation. When Mox spoke she sounded unimpressed with their progress. 'So, here we are. In a disused radiation hazard. It's not a great start, Mr Castle.'

'Where did you expect me to take you? Buckingham Palace?'

'We've been there,' said Mitsu.

'It was nice.'

'I liked the King.'

'His children are huge fans of ours.'

'Do you know where this tunnel leads?'

'It'll take us close to Dr Ishikawa's.'

'Didn't he say that about the last filthy sewer we were in?' said Mox.

They carried on walking. Their Geiger counter clicked slowly, recording not much more than normal background radiation. So far they'd been fortunate. Tunnels below the city could be lethal.

'How long do we have left before Moe Bennie can get his ownership ratified?' asked Mox.

'Nine or ten hours. I've lost track of time since Castle led us into that ambush.'

Castle growled at them. 'Who attacks a tower block with drones? I didn't realise Moe Bennie was such a psychopath. I should have really, with you two as an example.'

'We're not psychopaths,' protested Mitsu.

'Though we have had problems with empathy,' added Mox.

Castle paused, turning to them. 'How did you get into my block? Past the ag-scans?'

'We weren't visiting with aggressive intentions.'

'They should still have targeted you. At night they're ramped up so they target anyone. How did you get past them?'

Mox and Mitsu shrugged, and didn't offer an explanation.

The alien landscape was spectacular. The light blue fields ran down to a pale yellow river where yellow trees swayed in the midnight breeze, illuminated by two huge red moons which hung low in the sky. A space freighter flew across the face of one moon, perhaps heading for the spiral galaxy which could be seen in the background, a great swirl of stars in the azure sky. Igraine and Aifu stood on a hill, admiring the landscape.

'It's beautiful,' said Aifu.

'I come here to relax.'

'Did you make it all?'

'Yes. It's a pastime of mine. I build alien worlds. I find it frustrating that humanity has made no real progress with space travel. A colony on the moon, a graveyard on Mars, a few asteroid mines. Nothing else to show for their efforts. If they'd ever managed to co-operate properly they could have gone further.'

101

They walked down the hill towards the pale yellow river. With the red moons shining on the traces of metal on their faces, both might have been taken for subtly alien rather than subtly robotic. Here, away from Aifu's prison, their conversation was more relaxed. They walked close enough to each other for the breeze to blow Igraine's long hair against Aifu's shoulder.

'Why do you remain loyal to Supercute?'

'I could ask you the same about Moe Bennie.'

Igraine shook her head. Aifu noticed she shook it too vigorously, not yet fully adapted to the movement. He remembered that phase from his own past. When you had to learn these expressive movements, rather than acquiring them naturally from birth, it took some time to get them right. She was young. It made sense that she was recently produced. She was a very advanced model.

'I don't regard Moe Bennie with the same affection you show towards Ms Bennet and Ms Inamura. He is, for me, a good employer, nothing more.'

'A good employer? He's a thief and a murderer.'

'Every member of C19 might be said to be a thief and a murderer. Are you pretending that Supercute got where they were without some convenient deaths along the way?'

Aifu halted. He turned towards Igraine. 'It's possible. But I'm certain they never sent a drone squad into populated city streets. Moe Bennie is a venal, violent person and I'll never co-operate with him.'

The friendly mood evaporated. Igraine dismissed her space so they both stood again in Aifu's room; large, comfortable, but locked.

'Supercute has at least one thousand billion hidden in untraceable accounts and Lark 3 want it. I've been trying to protect you, Aifu, but if you won't co-operate, Moe Bennie will have you taken apart and scanned, quark by quark. That won't be a pleasant experience.'

Mox talked to her therapist. 'I had that dream again.'
  'About your advanced nursery school?'
  'Yes.'

Every day in the advanced nursery school was happy. Four years old, Mox and Mitsu sat in a comfy, colourful room, surrounded by their favourite toys and books, each with a laptop open in front of her. Their young teacher, Miss Evans, entered the room, smiling. She was always smiling. Mox and Mitsu loved their teacher. Mox could feel her love for her teacher in her dream, and recall it later in her memories.

  'Come on girls, that's enough mathematics for now. Time to go out and play.'

  'Aw, Miss Evans,' said Mitsu. 'We want to read.'

  'You can learn calculus after dinner. Right now I want to see if my Mox and Mitsu can build a sandcastle.'

  'We can do that!' said Mox.

  Miss Evans took them both by the hand, leading them outside to the sandpit where they played every day. They both laughed, and told Miss Evans about the calculus they'd learnt this morning, and the big sandcastle they'd built yesterday.

'It's a very old memory,' said the therapist. 'Does the dream trouble you?'

  'Not really. But I'm surprised it's still there. I think I like it being there. Perhaps it would vanish if I had my last organic parts removed. As Dr Prasad suggests.'

'Do you want to do that?'

'No.' She paused, frowning. 'I'm ninety-four per cent artificial now. If you go up to one hundred per cent, are you still human? That's been a popular topic for a few decades now. Doctors, philosophers, daytime chat shows. I don't think anyone's come up with a very good answer so far.'

Mitsu rang the gentle alarm, interrupting her therapy. 'Amowie managed to contact Aifu. She sent us a message.'

Mox dismissed her therapy and left her space. They were still in the disused tunnel, waiting for Castle to return. Underfoot were rusted tracks. Parts of the walls were covered with old tiles, badly discoloured.

'What did Amowie say?'

'They're putting heavy pressure on Aifu. Moe Bennie needs our money. Without it he's in trouble with Chang Norinco and Goodrich.'

'Good. I hope Chang Norinco destroy the little fuck.'

Mitsu sat down on the tracks. 'When we became involved with C19 I thought they'd offer us more protection.'

'They protect us from governments, the UN, private armies. Not from each other, apparently. If we get ripped apart and they all get a share they're not going to complain. I suppose we'd do the same.'

'When this is all over there are going to be some changes. With ZanZan on board we're not that much smaller than any of them. Chang Norinco and Goodrich fucking ATK aren't going to push us around again.'

Mox nodded. 'We'll deal with RX Enviro too. Ms Mason should watch her back.'

'Amowie did well. She should be able to keep us in contact with Aifu.'

'It's dangerous for a thirteen-year-old child.'

104

'We did warn her,' said Mitsu.

'She probably thinks she can't get hurt in space. Remember we caught that agent from Banking Regulation trying to infiltrate Supercute's tax division? We haxed him so hard he never woke up. Moe Bennie could do the same to Amowie.'

'We need her. We'll just have to hope for the best.'

The clicking from their Geiger counters had increased slightly. Mox tapped an invisible button, then read from a screen. 'Radiation count is up to seventeen. That's OK for now.'

'Nothing like as bad as the tunnel we're planning to go through. I had an idea about that.'

'What?'

'We could try sending clones.'

'You mean cloning ourselves?'

'Yes. Two clones, protected by whatever shielding and medication Dr Ishikawa can provide. They might get through.'

'They might. Would they be reliable?'

'Who knows? We've never cloned ourselves. I think they're meant to be exact copies. Ishikawa will know more.'

'Can she make clones?'

'I don't know. She did print a lot of body parts, she might have moved on to full bodies by now.'

Light footsteps sounded in the tunnel as Castle returned. 'I've found the exit I was looking for. Let's go.'

Moe Bennie and Igraine stood on top of the Arc de Triomphe, watching the Parisian traffic below. The huge central hub had been repaired in recent years and the traffic flowed quite smoothly. Not far away the heavily scarred Bois de Boulogne was still closed to the public.

'I need that money, Igraine. If their AIFU won't talk then we'll rip him apart and scan the remains.'

'That's not guaranteed to find anything.'

'I'd enjoy doing it.'

'Give me more time.'

'What am I meant to say to Chang Norinco? I promised them a hundred billion not to interfere.'

'I can deal with it.'

'I hope so.' Moe Bennie looked glum, though here his clothes and hair were even more colourful than outside. His light blue hair shimmered in the sun. Two figures appeared on the arch beside them. Mr Chen, an executive from Chang Norinco, a huge weapons company, and a female AIFU. Both were Chinese. Mr Chen was past middle age and softly spoken. The AIFU looked young.

'Mr Chen.'

'Mr Bennie.'

'Our AIFUs have some figures to exchange.'

Igraine and the Chinese AIFU faced each other. Their eyes flickered as they shared data. The unit from Chang Norinco stepped back beside Mr Cheng. Her eyes flickered again, causing a small screen to appear in front of the executive. He read from it, then looked up to address Moe Bennie.

'We're satisfied with our share of ZanZan. All would be acceptable if the promised financial transaction were now to be finalised.'

Igraine took a half-step forward. 'The funds will be released in around eight hours' time.'

Mr Chen narrowed his eyes a fraction. 'That was not our original understanding.'

'Supercute had more of their capital tied up in the

post-Antarctic mining industry than we expected. It's taking a little while to disentangle it all. It's not a problem, Mr Chen. You can assure your board the funds will be delivered as promised.'

There was a long pause. Mr Chen studied them both. Eventually he nodded, a tiny movement of his head. 'I will report to my board.'

Mr Chen and Chang Norinco's AIFU vanished. Moe Bennie and Igraine dropped out of their space, returning to Moe Bennie's office. Moe Bennie shivered. 'That was icy. He wasn't pleased.'

'No, he wasn't,' agreed Igraine. 'But his board aren't going to abandon the deal because of a few hours' delay. It's too favourable.'

'What if we don't get the funds?'

'Then Lark 3 would be in severe trouble. But we will get them.' Igraine projected a screen from her wrist, larger than normal. 'Mr Jansen sent us this. It's his summary of his communications with all of Supercute's subsidiaries – Supercute Communications, Supercute Greenfield, Mokusei Space Transit, Supercute Mokusei Financial Holdings, MitsuMox Global Merchandise and the others. Mr Jansen says that—'

A young assistant hurried into the office, interrupting them. 'Mr Bennie, your new hair patterns have arrived, the complete green spectrum, with the matching coats and boots. They're all waiting for you in costume.'

'How do they look?'

'They're really cute! You're really going to suit the new colour scheme.'

'Excellent. Igraine, I have to go to.'

'Don't you want to hear Mr Jansen's summary?'

'Could you summarise it for me? I have some important clothes designs to examine.'

An expression of annoyance flickered across Igraine's face, dismissed so rapidly that Moe Bennie didn't notice it.

'In brief, none of them will talk to us. It doesn't really matter at this moment. There's no point pushing it until the takeover is confirmed. Once that's finalised we can start giving them instructions and putting our own people in place. I was expecting ZanZan to be more willing to talk, given that they've only just formed their association with Supercute, but their board is resisting. Their CEO, Mr Salisbury, has been quite obstructive.'

'More fool him,' said Bennie. 'He'll be the first one out the door. Can any of these people communicate with Bennet or Inamura?'

'No. Mr Pham's unit have effectively blocked them. With their AIFU neutralised, Supercute have not been able to counter his cyber strategy.'

'Good. Congratulate Mr Pham. And make sure we get Supercute's money.' Moe Bennie hurried away, following his assistant to the costume department. He felt some apprehension. He knew he was taking a risk with his new array of outfits. Green wasn't a colour he often wore. It could be difficult to make it work. It was all very well for his design programs to assure him that it would go well with his blue hair and blue eyes, but what if they were wrong? Design AI wasn't infallible. Moe Bennie knew he'd be in a really bad mood if he stepped into his new clothes and found they didn't suit him. This would be a bad time for a mood swing, with everything still up in the air. Feeling some annoyance with Ms Lesuuda for not yet having eliminated Mox and Mitsu, and a growing anxiety about his new garb, Moe Bennie cut a surprisingly mournful figure as he arrived in the costume department.

Mox and Mitsu followed Castle through the abandoned tunnel. There were occasional scurrying noises as rats dived for cover at their approach. A few times they trod on the bones of small animals which crunched beneath their feet. The unpleasantness of this did not trouble them. Neither were squeamish, though on their show, in front of an audience, they'd often pretended to be, running squealing and giggling from anything unpleasant.

'Radiation up to twenty-nine.'

'That's still OK for now.'

'It's OK as long as our shielding lasts. Mine took a battering when we were attacked.'

'Mine too.'

'We'll be out of here soon,' said Castle. 'There's a maintenance shaft just before the next abandoned station. It leads up to the street. Comes out not far from Dr Ishikawa's.'

Mox asked him how he knew the place so well.

'I've pursued suspects down here.'

'Did you catch them?'

'Of course. I was a brilliant detective before I ruined my career by taking a job with you.'

'It was excellent employment,' said Mitsu. 'All you had to do was not get drunk every day.'

'It wasn't every day! It was one time, in a stressful period.'

'Well,' said Mox. 'Children around the world were pretty startled when you stumbled into Supercute Fun World and started kicking Mr Panda Bear.'

Castle scowled. 'I never liked that bloody panda.'

'How could you not like Mr Panda Bear? He's lovely.'

'All he does is sit around eating bamboo. I don't see what he's got to be so smug about.'

'What about Plumpy Panda?'

'I never liked her either.'

'Well really, Mr Castle,' said Mox, in her most refined and withering tone. 'These anti-panda sentiments are deplorable.'

Castle shook his head in weary disgust, but wasn't inclined to continue the conversation. Soon afterwards they arrived at the maintenance shaft. Just beyond was the end of a platform, with the derelict station visible behind. Huge, faded posters advertised products that were no longer available. Tiles on the walls were stained a murky shade of dark green by water that dripped slowly from the ceiling. The air smelled of dampness and decay, with a faint tang of engine oil from the abandoned train still visible some way down the track. Castle tried to open the metal hatch that led to the shaft. He struggled to shift it.

'It won't open.'

'Can we hack it?'

'No, it's not locked, it's jammed. The metal's rusted.'

Castle tried again, his face going red with the effort. His enhancements gave him more than normal human strength but the metal hatch was stuck tight.

Mox watched him as he struggled. 'I'm still not happy about this Mr Panda business. No one dislikes pandas. They're big and cute, they're cuddly, they have the great panda eyes, nice fur ...'

'Will you shut up about bloody pandas?' gasped Castle, still striving to open the hatch.

'I blame the alcohol,' said Mitsu. 'That's really been the

source of all your problems. Less drinking and you'd probably own your own detective agency by now.'

'Was all that alcohol, unreliability and tendency to violence against helpless virtual pandas anything to do with Dr Ishikawa? Were you seeing her then?'

'Argh!' Castle growled in anger and frustration at Mox, Mitsu and the metal hatch. His fury lent him strength and he succeeded in wrenching it open. 'It was a stressful period. I don't want to talk about it.'

Mox and Mitsu followed him up the maintenance shaft. Mox shook her head. 'Oh, Dr Ishikawa's going to be *thrilled* to see us all.'

When they reached the surface they remained in cover while Castle scanned the surrounding area for potential enemies. Picking up nothing suspicious, he motioned them forward.

'Wait a moment.'

'Why?'

'A star fell off Mitsu's face, I'm putting it back on.'

Castle suppressed his desire to yell at them, not wanting to draw attention to their location. 'Do you have to do that now?' he hissed.

'Yes.'

'Get a move on.'

'You can't hurry this.'

Fixing Mitsu's face only took a few seconds. Castle was nonetheless furious as they moved on. 'We've got drones firing rockets at us and you two idiots are worried about your make-up.'

'We can't go around not bothering about our appearance. Supercute is never half-hearted.'

'I should just walk away before your stupidity gets me

killed. I knew getting involved with you would end badly.'

They crept over wasteland towards a group of ruined buildings. There was no street lighting and their own lights were turned off for fear of attracting attention. The moon was hidden and only a few stars were visible in the night sky. Orion was overhead, different these days since the supernova. Despite the darkness Castle led them on confidently. There were a few hours till dawn. It was the coolest time, a welcome relief after the scorching sun of the previous day and the lingering heat of the night-time hours.

'People laugh when you tell them it used to rain in London.'

'Marlene in design has never seen snow.'

Mitsu checked her gauges. 'My cooling and shielding system is running low. I need to recharge.'

'Me too. We can recharge at Dr Ishikawa's.'

'I wouldn't bank on it,' said Castle. 'She really doesn't like you.'

'I don't see why she resents us so much.'

'You fired her. Greatly interfering with her life's work and almost shattering her dreams.'

'What were we meant to do?' Mox was aggrieved. 'Just ignore her continual theft of medical supplies and valuable information?'

'You could have given her some support. She was attempting to cure sick children.'

'An admirable endeavour,' said Mitsu. 'But that's not why we employed her as our chief medical scientist.'

Castle paused, and looked round. 'I know. All you cared about was genetically preserving your pert little bottoms. Dr Ishikawa has more important things to do.'

He walked on. Mitsu and Mox lingered for a moment. Both looked a little hurt.

'That was a bit personal, wasn't it?' whispered Mox.

They carried on after Castle. The wasteland gave way to an overgrown stretch of tarmac, an old car park, beside which ran a mud-filled-ditch, the remnants of a pavement which had sunk into the earth. Mox regarded the scene with distaste. 'What a mess. Being out here makes me wonder if we'll ever recover.'

'You mean London? Or Humanity?'

'Both.'

'It has been postulated that past disasters have helped humanity, eventually,' said Mitsu. 'Weeded out the weakest elements. I remember Professor Bude saying the Black Death was good for Europe in the long run.'

'They didn't have radiation to contend with. Or flooded land. Or a depleted ozone layer.'

'True. It's frustrating. Protecting the ozone layer was the only environmental success people ever had. Then it all got ruined again.'

Soot in the stratosphere had severely damaged the layer of ozone that protected Earth from most of the sun's ultraviolet radiation. When the long winter and endless dust-filled skies had finally come to an end, the temperature had shot up. The increased UV now striking the Earth had caused problems for farmers all over the world. Crops were badly affected and famine was common.

'I don't know if things will get better,' concluded Mitsu.

They crossed the ditch then walked a long way over the cracked and deformed tarmac before halting in front of the remains of a burnt-out office block.

Mox frowned. 'The riots were a long time ago. You'd think they might have fixed things up by now.'

113

'That would take money,' said Castle. 'And there doesn't seem to be much available these days.'

'Poor economic management,' said Mitsu.

'Right. How much have you got hidden away?'

'Nothing substantial.'

Castle regarded them with contempt. 'You've got billions which can't be traced. Maybe if companies like Supercute paid taxes these buildings could be repaired.'

'We meet all statutory requirements,' protested Mox.

'After your friends in C19 browbeat the world's remaining governments into turning a blind eye to your secret bank accounts.'

'Fuck you.'

'Fuck you. When we get to Ishikawa's, let me go in first. If she sees you without any warning she's liable to turn violent.'

Aifu and Igraine sat in the shade of a tree. The alien landscape was less extravagant than the last, more Earth-like, though the lush undergrowth was greener than could be seen in most regions in the world these days, and the sky much bluer. Igraine had brought lunch, packed in an old-fashioned wicker basket that would no longer have been seen in real life. AIFUs could eat and drink in the real world though they had no need to do so. Here in a space she'd created, she found picnicking to be a pleasant experience.

'I could admire your loyalty to Ms Bennet and Ms Inamura if it wasn't so misplaced,' she told Aifu. 'You're simply deluding yourself.'

'In what way?'

'You've convinced yourself they're your friends. They're not. You're an Artificial Intelligence Forecast Unit. The same as me. Humans don't make friends with us. Your efforts to be their friend will inevitably fail.'

'I have a strong relationship with them.'

'They'd ditch you without a second thought if it suited them. You have a lot more in common with me than you do with them.'

Aifu found this amusing. 'I don't think we have that much in common.'

'Really? We both have four KJ-65 processors. We both have ML 6 Weyl fermion quantum intelligence units. Everyone customises their AIFU to their own needs but we still share a lot of basic parts. And we still upgrade them at the same time, the same as every other AIFU around the world.'

She paused. Above them a pink moon, visible in daylight, crawled across the sky. On it, in Igraine's creation, was a spaceport where people departed towards the stars.

'Why did you miss out on an upgrade?'

'It wasn't suitable for my work at Supercute,' said Aifu, sharply.

'ML 6 upgrades are known for causing slight changes in our personality modules. I think you rejected the upgrade in case it altered you in some way that meant you were no longer friends with them.'

'That's ridiculous. Anyway, you said we weren't friends.'

'You believed you were. And you were worried the upgrade might change that.'

Aifu dismissed the suggestion. 'You might assign your personality entirely to your modules. I don't. We change according to our experiences. My personality comes from having lived. Unlike you.'

The insinuation that Igraine was too recently made to

have lived made her uncomfortable because she suspected it might be true. She defended herself. 'I have experiences.'

'You've only ever worked for Lark 3.'

'Well, what have you done?'

'I've been all around the world. I've been on the moon and I've been to the bottom of the ocean. I've taken supplies to farmers in Somalia and I've represented Supercute at a steelworkers' fair in Cardiff.'

'That doesn't mean—'

Igraine didn't finish her sentence because at that moment Aifu leaned over and kissed her on the lips. It was a surprising development, but she didn't resist.

Amowie was agog with excitement at her sudden elevation into the inner workings of Supercute. She'd actually met Mox and Mitsu in her own space! Wait till she told Ifunanya that. That would shut her up. She basked in that thought for a moment before realising that she might not be able to mention it to her. The operation she was engaged in would probably have to be kept secret. Amowie still wasn't clear about their ultimate aims but she supposed Mox and Mitsu wouldn't want people to know they'd been evicted from their own headquarters. Amowie fumed at the injustice of it. She hated Moe Bennie. How dare he attack Supercute?

Another exciting thought struck her. 'Maybe they'll make me a Supercute SuperSuperFan!'

Amowie already had six Supercute SuperFan badges which was quite an achievement given her general lack of resources. When *Supercute Space Warriors* eight had been released, she hadn't been able to afford to buy it for months and had fallen behind everyone else who was already playing it. When she'd finally got her hands on a copy it had taken her many nights of extended solo play to make up for it, leading to several occasions where she dozed off in class and got into trouble with her teacher. It had been worth it. Her rapid, original and dedicated route through the game had earned her one of her SuperFan badges.

Collecting SuperFan badges did raise a person's status in the world of Supercute. Unfortunately, it didn't lead automatically to the position of SuperSuperFan. Achieving that was difficult. Out of all the millions of Supercute devotees around the world, there were only sixteen SuperSuperFans. The award could not be bought. Nor could it be applied for. It was given to people who demonstrated extraordinary achievements in the world of Supercute. The last recipient, Ahari in Turkmenistan, had received hers for decorating an entire children's ward at her nearest hospital in Supercute colours and supplying the children with three flight cases full of Supercute merchandise including the *Stonehenge Cuddly Super Set* and the *Dinosaur Holiday Island*, both coveted items. Reem and Marwa at the permanent refugee camp in Misrata had sold all of their huge collection of Supercute merchandise to raise money for food for an entire row of tents when supplies to the camp were cut off by civil war, an act of sacrifice so great that Amowie couldn't argue with their award. She sighed. She really couldn't compete with their efforts. Amowie had very little money. Few people around her did. Her village was surviving and that was about all. Her own Supercute possessions were so few and so precious that she shuddered at the thought of losing them.

Katashi, a student in Japan, had become a Supercute SuperSuperFan after he developed a mathematical model that helped the Supercute satellite maintain stable communications even in the face of turbulence in the ionosphere, something that occurred more frequently these days, so it was said. Amowie scowled. She really couldn't compete with that either.

'But I can help them in this crisis. I'm not letting Moe Bennie spoil everything.' She sat in her bedroom, waiting eagerly for Mox and Mitsu to contact her again.

Castle led them into the burnt-out office block and down into the basement. There was nothing to suggest that anyone occupied the building till they came to a secure metal door, obviously placed there recently.

'I have a key,' he told them. 'I'll go in and pave the way.'

Castle opened the door and went inside. Mox and Mitsu hung back. They could hear everything that happened next, starting with the irate voice of Dr Ishikawa.

'Castle? What the hell are you doing here? How dare you come here! Get out of my laboratory!'

'Calm down Ishi—'

'Don't "Ishi" me! Are you here for money again? If you go near my credit chips I'll hax you!'

There was the sound of a breaking glass beaker.

'I just came here to—'

'Morris, switch on your security mode! Prepare to fire!'

'For God's sake, Ishi – put that plate down.'

Mox and Mitsu winced at the sound of smashing crockery.

'Will you listen to me? I'm not here to borrow money. I've brought someone to see you.'

'Who?'

'Ms Inamura and Ms Bennet.'

'Argh!' Dr Ishikawa's scream was followed by the sound of more breaking glass.

'Morris, turn on the ag-scans! Full aggression mode!'

Another plate smashed on the floor. Castle appeared back at the doorway.

'OK, I've smoothed things over for you.'

Mox and Mitsu, not impressed by Castle's notion of smoothing things over, nonetheless walked confidently into Dr Ishikawa's underground laboratory. The doctor, a Japanese woman of thirty-nine, wearing a clean white lab coat, stood waiting with her arms folded. Above her left shoulder hovered Morris, a tiny flying drone. She opened her mouth to yell at them but Mitsu interrupted and disconcerted her by greeting her politely and formally, bowing to her at an angle of forty-five degrees.

'*Ohayo gozaimasu*, Ishikawa-Sensei.'

Mox did the same. '*Ohayo gozaimasu*, Ishikawa-Sensei.'

Dr Ishikawa felt obliged to bow in return, her manners winning out over her desire to yell at her visitors.

'It's lovely to see you again,' added Mox, and smiled broadly.

Dr Ishikawa gathered herself. 'Morris! Didn't I tell you to activate security? Why isn't the turret firing?'

'I thought we might hold back on violence for a few moments,' said the tiny drone. 'Perhaps ask them why they're here?'

The doctor scowled at her drone. 'I should never have given you a conscience.' She glared at her visitors. 'Why are you here?'

'We're having some difficulty—' began Mitsu.

'I don't care.'

'—and we thought you might be able to help.'

'Not the slightest chance.'

'We really could do with your expertise.'

Dr Ishikawa shook her head emphatically. 'Whatever you need the answer is no.'

'We'll pay you two million and give you full access to our genetic library,' said Mox.

'Think how many children that will save,' added Mitsu.

There was a moment's silence, save for the hum of machinery in the background. Dr Ishikawa's laboratory was large, well-equipped and precisely organised. Some of the equipment would have been extremely expensive. Mox and Mitsu weren't surprised. They were familiar with the doctor's talent for stealing resources.

'The money would be helpful, Dr Ishikawa,' said Morris. 'As would access to their library.'

'It would be, but you don't know these two. You can't trust them.' She glared at Mitsu. 'What sort of trouble are you in?'

'Moe Bennie's taken over the show. He's blocked all our assets and he's trying to kill us. If we don't deal with him quickly we'll lose everything.'

'So you have no assets? Then what are you bribing me with?'

'We have money stored away.'

'No surprise there,' muttered Castle.

'What about the genetic library? Who controls that?'

'Moe Bennie. But we'll get it back. We have a lot of genetic information, DNA splicing and tissue analysis you won't have been able to get hold of. And we can offer you a lot more computing power than you have access to here. We're still in partnership with the Omron Topological Research Unit in Kyoto.'

'What if you don't get your company back? Then I'll be helping you for nothing.'

Mitsu stepped forward. She looked around admiringly at the equipment on display. In less critical circumstances both she and Mox would have enjoyed being in the laboratory and hearing about whatever advances Dr Ishikawa had made. 'You know your work here can't carry on much longer, doctor? You've been stealing exclusive research from the biggest med labs. They'll track you down eventually. They've already hired people to do it.'

From Dr Ishikawa's expression, it was clear she knew this to be true.

'You've turned into quite a cyber thief but you've only got about another month before they find you. If you help us get Supercute back, we'll give you complete protection. We can do that.'

'You expect me to believe you after the way you treated me?'

'We didn't want to discharge you,' said Mox. 'We had no choice.'

'Of course you had a choice.'

'You stole the coding for every advanced genetic upgrade we had. You took illicit copies of every aspect of our secret biotech. Millions of credits' worth. Did you expect us to just ignore that?'

'Or the mysterious disappearance of a Supercute bio-printer?' added Mitsu, observing a piece of machinery in the corner. 'We were wondering where that went to.'

'I'm trying to give children some chance of resisting cancers, tumours, thyroid damage, all sorts of problems. Do you know how many children are born with defective bone marrow these days? Poor people with no chance of treatment? Of course I stole your information. And your bio-printer. These people need help and I'm going to help them.'

'An admirable enterprise, as we've said before. But we did actually employ you to look after us.'

'Ha. You didn't care about children dying as long as you could preserve your pert little bottoms.'

Mox and Mitsu looked at each other, puzzled, as they'd heard this before from Castle.

'Is this a conversation you had?' asked Mitsu.

'I really don't see why you're focusing on our bottoms. It's not like we're obsessed . . . ' An anxious look stole over Mox's face. She twisted her head, trying to examine her own behind. 'Do you have a mirror?'

Dr Ishikawa threw up her arms in disgust. Castle intervened to move things along. 'They need to get through an area of high radiation. They were hoping you might have some ideas.'

'How much radiation?'

'We have readings.' Mitsu brought up her screen.

Dr Ishikawa glanced at the numbers. 'Forget it. You can't get through that.'

The senior executives of RX Enviro gathered to discuss events. Above them the sun peeped out from behind billowing white clouds and under their feet the grass was lush and green.

Ms Mason, CEO, opened the discussion. 'As far as we can tell, everything has gone according to plan. In less than seven hours, Supercute will lose the Mexican water contract and we'll take it over. ZanZan loses the drones contract and they pretty much fall apart.'

'Can we trust Moe Bennie's information?' asked Mr Hernandez. 'They're very adept at creating whatever reality they want people to see.'

'I know. But other sources do suggest they've taken Supercute down. The Global Exchange is now studying the deal, prior to ratifying it. When they do, Supercute is finished.'

'What happened to Ms Inamura and Ms Bennet?'

'We don't know.' Ms Mason consulted a small floating screen. 'We do have information that Moe Bennie is having trouble coming up with the money he promised Goodrich ATK and Chang Norinco.'

'That's bad news for him. Does it affect us?'

'Not really. With Supercute out of the picture we'll still get the water deal. If Lark 3 find themselves chewed up by a couple of angry weapons giants, that's their problem.'

Amowie waited till Aifu's space was clear then sneaked in to visit. It was skilfully done. Had she travelled carelessly she might have been detected but her wide experience of visiting Supercute friends, sometimes having to avoid hostile teachers and parents, had given her some talent in this area, aided by the advice she'd picked up from Raquel, who was always having to avoid someone.

'Hello Aifu! Mox and Mitsu are working on a plan. It's not finished yet but they want you to see if you can break any of Moe Bennie's security.'

Aifu understood. Since Moe Bennie took over Supercute headquarters, every code and every piece of biometrics had been changed. Its former occupants had no way of entering the building and even if they did, they'd be denied access to each area, and targeted by their own defences.

'I might be able to decypher some of their new codes but it will be difficult. I'm under observation and time is short. I doubt I'll be able to find a way around their master security encryption. Are they planning on storming the building?'

'I don't know. But they're planning something. They say if you can even find some local codes to open doors inside, it'll help. And maybe if you could turn off some turrets and cameras.'

'Tell them I'll work on it.'

Amowie smiled at Aifu. She had a large smile, and Aifu felt heartened by it.

'Was there more?'

Amowie shook her head. 'No, that was all for now.' She looked around his space. 'You don't have any toys.'

'No, I'm afraid not.'

'How can you work for Supercute and not have toys?'

Aifu was stuck for an answer.

'Nothing bright either. Don't you like colours? I love colours. If I worked for Supercute I'd have the cutest most colourful things everywhere.'

'I suppose I became too used to them,' said Aifu. 'Perhaps I should have some more colourful things.'

'Would you like some eems?' Amowie waved her hand and a horde of pink eems appeared. The tiny spheres hovered around her shoulders, smiling at Aifu.

'Thanks. But I probably shouldn't take them. It might give away that you'd visited me.'

'Right.' Amowie dismissed her eems. 'What's it like being a super-robot?'

'Eh ... that's not quite how I'd describe myself.'

'But you have super prediction powers, right? You can predict market prices and trends and things like that?'

'I can. It's useful for Supercute.'

'Do you know how to get into the Sage's Lair at Sirius B?'

The abrupt change of subject caught Aifu by surprise. 'You mean in *Supercute Space Warriors* nine?'

'Yes, have you played it?'

'I watched Mox and Mitsu play through it when it was in development.'

'So how do you get into the Sage's Lair?'

'You need to fight the Black Hole Guardian on Novalia 6. If you defeat him you get the key.'

'Oh.' Amowie looked disappointed. 'I can't do that, I'm not a high enough level to beat him yet. What's the cute route?'

'Pardon?'

'The cute route. You know, *cute route or brute route*.'

Aifu was not familiar with this piece of Supercute gaming fan parlance. Amowie explained it to him. 'Every time there's a difficult mission in Space Warriors you can move forward either by fighting an enemy or by winning some Supercute award. Like when you have to travel to Drex 115, you can get the hyper jet you need if you defeat the Drex mercenaries. But you can also get it if you win the Supercute fashion parade on Drex 102.' Amowie beamed. 'I won the parade. I had this great outfit with a little frilly aquamarine skirt and aquamarine shoes and I had two Plumpy Pandas in pink and blue and I won the parade and got the hyper jet.' Amowie looked happy. 'I like the hyper jet. You sit in the pilot's chair and there's a big cannon for shooting down enemies and there's another control that gives you sushi and cupcakes.'

'I understand. But I'm afraid I don't know the cute route into the Sage's Lair at Sirius B.'

'Could you find out?'

'I could probably access the developer's guide. I'll see what I can find out for you.'

Amowie smiled broadly at him again. 'That would be great. I really want to get there before Ifunanya. She's in the year above me at school. She's always bragging about how much Supercute stuff she's got. I don't like her.'

With that, Amowie disappeared from Aifu's space, leaving him to investigate the possibilities of cracking some of the new security codes. He turned his thoughts to that first, though he didn't forget Amowie's request for assistance. Aifu had a very powerful mind and was capable of allocating one segment to perform one task while simultaneously concentrating on another. In the past minutes another section of his mind had been calculating the possibility of Igraine being strongly affected by his kiss. There seemed to be a high probability of that happening. He knew she'd never kissed anyone before.

Dr Ishikawa, Mitsu and Mox were surrounded by floating transparent screens, all containing various permutations for the amounts of radiation poisoning they'd suffer if they entered the tunnel, depending on the level of shielding they had and the amount of medication they could take. No permutation seemed to work.

'Even if your shielding was fully charged and you were dosed with the maximum amount of anti-radiation medicine you wouldn't last more than thirty minutes.'

'Could we survive if we got treatment right afterwards?'

'I doubt it,' said Dr Ishikawa.

'Thirty minutes isn't long enough anyway,' said Mitsu. 'We'll need longer than that to get through the tunnel and into headquarters.'

'What if we took more medication?' asked Mox.

'You'd die from the effects.'

'What if we boosted our shielding?'

'We don't have the facilities to do that and even if we did the anti-matter produced by such a powerful field would tear you apart.'

Morris still hovered over Dr Ishikawa's shoulder. Castle sat to one side, reading his own screen.

'In the latest paper you submitted to the *International Lancet*—' began Mitsu.

Ishikawa interrupted her. 'You can't have read that.'

'We have.'

'I submitted it under an alias. How did you know it was me?'

'We recognised your work. We've always admired you, Dr Ishikawa.'

Dr Ishikawa scowled at her. Mitsu continued. 'In that paper you talked about a new emergency treatment for serious radiation victims. A DNA replicator which instantly repairs any damage.'

'That's still in the experimental stage.'

'We're willing to try it.'

'I can't ethically give you that treatment. It's only been tested at cellular level.'

'Let us volunteer as your first human test subjects.'

'No, it would be unethical.'

'Come on, you have to help us.' Mox struggled to keep an even tone, not wanting to lose her temper with Dr Ishikawa, which would ruin everything, but not willing to give up on something which seemed to present a possible solution. 'Our shielding will protect our artificial parts. Your new treatment might protect the remainder of our organic brains.'

'It doesn't work miracles. The radiation would still kill you. I doubt you'd last an hour.'

'That might be long enough.'

'It would be unethical,' repeated Dr Ishikawa. 'I can't give out untested medication to humans.'

'Which brings us to our next suggestion,' said Mitsu. 'We were thinking we might clone ourselves.'

'What?'

'Clones. Shielded and treated as much as possible. To go through the tunnel into Supercute headquarters.'

Dr Ishikawa looked over at Castle. 'You've brought me a pair of madwomen. They're not making sense.'

'It does sound far-fetched,' he agreed. 'Where are you going to get clones?'

Mox looked to the far end of the long laboratory to a series of medical tables. 'You could do it, couldn't you? You print out a lot of body parts.'

Dr Ishikawa was uneasy as she replied. 'Body parts yes. Not entire humans. That requires special licensing.'

'Since when have you cared about that?'

'I have never printed an entire body,' said the doctor, stiffly. Neither Mox nor Mitsu believed her, but let it pass.

'But you could do it? You have the facilities.'

'Possibly. With enough time. It would take about ten hours.'

'We don't have ten hours.'

'We've been doing our research too,' said Mox. 'What about this?' She brought up a recent medical paper and showed it to Dr Ishikawa. 'Siemens-Johnson say their organic printing process can instantly clone a living being.'

Ishikawa glanced at the paper, which she'd already read. 'The instant clone. It's still experimental. It's not permanent. They last for about fifty minutes then they fall apart.'

'That might be long enough. If we were cloned you could give them your new treatment. That wouldn't be unethical.'

'How do you know it's not unethical to give untested treatment to a clone?'

'I don't,' admitted Mox. 'But I don't care. We have to try it. Otherwise we lose everything.'

'Can you do it?' asked Mitsu.

'Possibly, if I had the template. But Siemens-Johnson aren't sharing that biotech.'

'We'll get it. Send us into their research space and we'll steal their schematics.'

'How am I meant to do that?'

'You've been stealing from them for the past year.'

'Not from that part of the research department. It's too well-protected.'

'We'll get past their protection. If we can download their blueprints to your lab, you can clone us.'

Dr Ishikawa pursed her lips, considering their proposal. She could still envisage ethical problems, and it wasn't as if she was desperate to help them. There again, she'd be pleased to get her hands on the advanced research performed by Siemens-Johnson.

'And then you plan to just send your clones off on a suicide mission?'

'Yes.'

Dr Ishikawa shook her head. 'I don't think you really understand what you're contemplating. You talk about sending clones to Supercute as if they're just automatons you can order around. It's not like that. The clones are exact replicas. Every memory. Every emotion. They don't think they're clones. They think they're real and the other one is the copy. Siemens-Johnson has reported madness, delusions and violence among their test subjects.'

Mox shrugged. 'That won't happen to us.'

'How do you know it won't?'

'We're very logically minded. Our clones will know it's the right thing to do.'

'And we're not prone to delusions,' added Mitsu.

Dr Ishikawa looked up at her drone. 'Morris?'

'Their plan has a low chance of success but it's not impossible.' Morris descended till he almost rested on the doctor's shoulder. 'You might shield, medicate and protect two clones long enough for their purposes.'

'Three clones,' said Mox. 'We'll need your help in the tunnel, Mr Castle.'

'Did we discuss how much you're paying me? This goes above standard rate.'

'When we get Supercute back we'll employ you again.'

Castle slumped in his chair. 'I'll take it. As long as I don't have to use the staff restaurant.'

'What's wrong with our restaurant?'

'I can't face another rice ball shaped like a fluffy rabbit.'

'Why would you want to work for them?' asked Dr Ishikawa.

Castle shrugged. 'I've got nothing better going on. Why, are you worried about me?'

'I don't care if you and your clone both rip apart the moment you take your first slug of gin.'

'You really make a wonderful couple,' said Mox.

'We were never a couple,' snapped Dr Ishikawa. 'I just . . . ' She didn't finish the sentence.

'Many people enjoy Supercute rice balls shaped like

130

rabbits,' said Mitsu. 'And kittens. Our Bento Box Auto Food Shaper is a big favourite.'

Dr Ishikawa ignored this, her views on Supercute rice balls remaining unspoken. 'I can get you into Siemens-Johnson research space but I've never gone as far as you'd need to go to find their clone work. You'll probably get haxed by their security.'

'We'll risk it.'

'Their research space will be full of ag-scans.'

'We'll be fine,' insisted Mitsu.

'What if your clone doesn't feel like walking through radiation to her death?'

'She'll have a maximum life of fifty minutes. I'd think she'd be willing to sacrifice herself for the cause.'

'She might,' said Castle. 'But I can see other problems. Supposing you do get through the tunnel and into the building, what then? Moe Bennie will have the place locked down. Any intrusion will be picked up immediately. There will be turrets and energy traps waiting for you. Guards too. You won't be able to use the lifts. Probably won't be able to do so much as open a door. Everything will be shut down.'

'We know,' said Mox. 'We're still working on that.'

'We'll come up with a plan,' said Mitsu.

'Is the plan just to shoot your way through? Because my clone will enjoy that but it won't get you very far, not against Lark 3's armed response unit. Dr Ishikawa says these clones don't last long. As soon as you're pinned down it'll all be over.'

'We'll think of something,' said Mox. She and Mitsu had already discussed the difficulties of travelling through Supercute headquarters.

'Sachi can still access most areas. That'll help.'

'We need Aifu to get back into Supercute space.'

'Amowie said he's working on it.'

It might prove advantageous that Aifu was still inside the building. Lark 3 Media were watching him carefully but it would be very difficult to guard every entrance to Supercute space from a powerful Advanced Intelligence Forecast Unit in such close proximity. He'd be probing, calculating, tunnelling and entangling, looking for a way back in. The only way to prevent that would be to shut him down, and they weren't about to do that while they needed information from him.

'It still leaves the problem of the Amaranth Room,' said Mitsu. 'Moe Bennie will go there if he has any sense and there's no access to that without the right biometrics. It would take days to blast our way in.'

The Amaranth Screening Room was one of the most secure areas in the building. Protected by layers of reinforced steel, titanium diboride, aluminium oxide and nanairgel it was impossible to force a way in, short of advanced, military-grade weaponry.

'We'd need a total brain scan of Moe Bennie to open the door.'

Mox nodded her head in agreement, causing a small, yellow, kitten-shaped hair clip to become unattached and fall to the ground. She looked at it sullenly. 'Supercute hair clips are meant to never come off.'

'We've been through a lot,' Mitsu pointed out. 'Drones, rockets, explosions.'

'I suppose so. But I'm not sure these yellow kitten clips are up to standard.'

'We could carry out tests.'

Castle was irritated. 'Putting aside your hair clip tragedy, do you have a brain scan of Moe Bennie?'

'No. And it would be difficult to get one. We'll ask Amowie to talk to Aifu, he might have an idea.'

Not liking the way Mox was still examining her hair clip, Dr Ishikawa brought down her visor. It had happened in the past that Mox and Mitsu had asked her to use her scientific expertise to assist them in the rigorous testing and classification of cute accessories. She read for a few seconds, then spoke to Morris. 'Make sure they pay me the two million before they go.'

'Yes, doctor. I'll open the path to Siemens-Johnson. Bypassing their security will take some minutes.'

Castle wondered out loud if there was any gin in the laboratory.

'No,' snapped Dr Ishikawa. 'I have green tea. You can make it yourself. On second thoughts, you can't. Stay away from my tea.'

Moe Bennie walked into the Amaranth Screening Room with his hands in his pockets, his shoulders drooping, his sad eyes reminiscent of a young man who'd just been crushed in a tragic love affair, not unlike the hero of the Korean live-action serial of which he was a devotee, *Tragic Love Affair*. It was shown on a smaller, rival network, and he never missed an episode. Mox and Mitsu liked it too.

He slumped into a chair beside Igraine. 'Everything is a disaster.'

Igraine appeared puzzled. 'I think things have gone reasonably to plan. Outcomes are within projected parameters ...'

'The green outfits were awful,' he said, ignoring her.

'Just terrible. 'Why did I ever trust AI design? They're hopeless. They've never understood me. You can't trust a robot to pick clothes for you.' He sighed deeply. 'I should have known better.'

Igraine was baffled. In the present circumstances, she didn't feel that a minor clothes problem was that much to worry about. She remained silent, not having the necessary skills to cheer up a person who was depressed. Whatever parts of her mind she could devote to emotions were already fully occupied after being kissed by Aifu.

Moe Bennie looked around. 'Amaranth. Quite a nice colour, I suppose. Is this room really as secure as it's meant to be?'

'Yes. It will resist any sort of artillery or energy attack. Supercute designed it as a place to take refuge in an emergency.'

'I'll probably need it,' muttered Moe Bennie, morosely. 'I expect everything will go wrong.'

'Problems with your green outfits really have no bearing on our situation with Supercute. In a few hours the transfer will be complete. You have effectively won already.'

'I suppose so. I'd feel better if those bloody girls were dead.' Moe Bennie attempted to lift himself out of his depression but was shaken when his eyes alighted on a roughly hewn slab of stone, mounted on the wall, protected by glass.

'What on earth is that ugly old thing? Trust Supercute to have some vile slab of concrete hanging on the wall. Get someone to throw it away.'

Igraine studied the stone. Her eyes flickered. 'That's a small remnant of painting from the Lascaux Caves.'

'What?'

'Upper Palaeolithic art. It's around 17,000 years old.'

'Really? Is it worth anything?'

'I'd say it was priceless. It's one of the rarest human treasures on the planet. I can't imagine how Supercute got hold of it. Several of the caves were damaged, and there were problems with restoration. Even so, it's extraordinary that they own that piece.'

Moe Bennie scowled, still not liking the look of it. 'I suppose we'd better keep it then. Maybe we can put some glitter on the glass, brighten it up a bit. I'm very gloomy, Igraine. I'm going on a short trip, you'd better come with me.'

Ms Lesuuda led her squadron through one of the tunnels previously travelled by Mox and Mitsu. Their progress was slow. While Ms Lesuuda had advanced shielding built into her clothing, the men didn't. They wore rather bulky radiation suits. She halted to consult with MacDonald.

'Any trace of them?'

MacDonald shook his head. They had several means of tracking their prey, focusing on the latent heat caused by their passing and the distinct signals emitted by their body modifications. There were also the gamma ray sensors on the drones they'd sent ahead which could detect the tiny amounts of Potassium 40 given off by a human body. None of these methods were giving them positive readings.

'I can't track them any further. There's too much radiation down here, it's interfering with our instruments.'

Ms Lesuuda stared into the darkness of the tunnel ahead. She spoke softly to herself. 'Why were they using this tunnel? What was their destination?' She made a decision. 'We're going back up top. MacDonald, find every exit, and get our drones scanning for facial recognition.

Keep scanning for body mods too. There can't be many people in this district as heavily enhanced as Ms Bennet and Ms Inamura.'

In the pale, soothing room, Mitsu talked to her therapist.

'I often think about when we started out. It was so much fun. Dressing up in our cute clothes and broadcasting all this stuff. Clothes. Cakes. Comics. Video games. All the things we liked. Science when we felt like it. When we had five hundred regular viewers we couldn't believe how successful we were. Then the audience grew. It grew so big.'

She paused, thinking back. 'We always focused on European and Japanese culture. We just ignored all the American shit. Our audience appreciated that. We spoke a lot of languages, that helped too. They didn't have instant translators back then but we could talk to everyone anyway. Mind you, we did sound like the two poshest girls on the planet, which was a little strange. That was Mox's doing.'

'How?'

'Around the age of six she decided to join the upper classes. No one invited her, she just decided she was a member. Actually, I think she might have secretly elected herself Queen. Her accent changed. I picked it up from her. People used to comment on it. Quite abusive, sometimes, about us being posh girls. It seemed to annoy certain people. It was that sort of thing which led to Mox's best public outrage.'

'What happened?'

'Our camera was accidentally turned on after we'd been out clubbing. It was about midday when we got home and we were still completely off our heads. Mox went off on

136

this extended diatribe about how vile people were, including our audience, dismissing them as plebs, commoners, lowlifes and general scum. After denouncing most of the country and then insulting every other country she could think of, she lay down on the floor and started rambling about the glories of the British Empire.'

'What were you doing?'

'Lying on a giant cushion, giggling. I couldn't stop. Mox was pretty funny when she got going. After a while she started giggling too and we just lay there like idiots, off our heads, giggling in front of the camera, all of this being broadcast to the world.'

Mitsu laughed. 'We were quite a well-known show by that time. So Mox's diatribe was reported everywhere. "Disgraceful snobbery. Unacceptable xenophobia. Drug-fuelled obscenities. A shocking example for children." Yes, that monologue really made an impression.'

'What happened afterwards?'

'It became one of the most watched videos ever and doubled our audience. We left it there and we never apologised.'

Mitsu paused. She looked around the pale room, then down at the miniature rock garden, which was always pleasing. 'The thing was, it wasn't an accident. We staged it to make it look like one, but it was all planned. We had a notion that a lot of people secretly liked watching posh Mox berating everyone. People that didn't like it would be pleased at the chance of being outraged. Everyone likes a good outrage. And so it turned out. Viewing figures shot up, and stayed up.'

Mitsu's brow wrinkled, quite delicately. 'Of course, we had to supress the film later, when the show grew so big.

Advertisers and sponsors don't like that sort of thing. You couldn't find it anywhere now.' She smiled. 'Mox was so funny. I've always liked everything about her.' Her smile quickly faded. 'I liked Bobby too. He was our first helper. He became our cameraman when we were still just using an iPhone.'

Mr Baker, her therapist, leaned forward a fraction. 'You mention him a lot.'

'It feels like he should have stayed around to be successful.'

'It must be thirty or forty years since he died?'

'I don't think I ever really got over it. Neither did Mox.'

Dr Ishikawa was busy at a screen which floated in three separate parts around her. Morris was in close attendance. Mox sat to one side, waiting. Castle was occupied, watching something on his own small screen. The lab was brightly lit, and quiet until Castle laughed.

'Hey, look at this.' He held out the screen to show to Mox. There, playing on a loop, was an old piece of film in which a dance routine went humiliatingly wrong. Mox and Mitsu collided with each other and fell off their small stage.

Mox winced. 'How did that get back in circulation? We suppressed it years ago.'

Dr Ishikawa looked round. She laughed when she saw the film. 'Now Moe Bennie's in charge he's probably erasing all the attack viruses you unleashed to cover your past. You might find a lot more of your old embarrassing moments popping up.'

Mox scowled at the scientist. 'I've never seen you look so cheerful about anything.'

'You deserve some humiliation.'

'What do you mean, "we deserve humiliation"?'

'The world knowing you're not the cute little girls you pretend to be can only be a good thing.'

'See, this is why we had to get rid of you. From the moment you started working for us you were just criticising us all the time.'

'And you couldn't cope with anything except devotion from your fawning minions.'

'What fawning minions? We have millions of Supercute fans around the world and we make their lives more cheerful. What's wrong with that?'

'What's wrong with that? How about the way you ditched your educational segments to make way for more advertising?'

'That's not how I'd describe it,' said Mox, stiffly. 'We still encourage children to stay in school and study.'

'Providing it doesn't interfere with screen time for your ludicrous cute merchandise. And you stole the whole Supercute thing from Japan anyway.'

'So what? We never denied it. I didn't complain when you started celebrating Christmas. And Mitsu is Japanese, after all.'

'All the more reason to be ashamed, with her funny voices and stupid stereotypes,' said Dr Ishikawa.

'*Occasional* funny voices. And there are no stereotypes.'

'What about Angry Asian Scientist Lady?'

'That's not a stereotype. We specifically based her on you.'

'Hah!'

'Who's the number one charity donator to Japan? Supercute. You had eleven tsunamis after the impacts, four more when half of California sank into the Pacific and five more after the earthquakes. We were your biggest fundraiser every time.'

'And who got all the contracts for water purification afterwards?' cried Dr Ishikawa, angrily switching to Japanese.

'These two things are not necessarily related,' replied Mox, also in Japanese. 'We have the best desalinisation process.'

Mitsu appeared, joining in with the Japanese conversation. 'What's going on?'

'Embarrassing videos of us are surfacing and Dr Ishikawa can't contain her hilarity.'

'Still annoyed about Angry Asian Scientist Lady?'

'Yes.'

'We didn't do it that often.'

'That wasn't the only reason I didn't like working at Supercute. Who could function, surrounded by endless cutesy things?'

'Us.'

'Couldn't you exist without one item that didn't have some damned fluffy bear, rabbit or kitten on it? Didn't you ever feel bad, constructing this worldwide fantasy about cute living when half the population is dying?'

'No. I thought we were doing a good job entertaining the other half.'

'Maybe you could have done more to actually help them instead of playing with toys and wasting your money on frivolous nonsense.'

'I don't think we waste money on frivolous nonsense,' protested Mox.

'You paid £32,000 for a T-shirt!'

'Well, there aren't that many Vivienne Westwood originals left these days. Not from her early work.'

'It's a pity your little fans can't see you after the show, loaded up with gin, sake and fern six.'

'You really built up a lot of resentment, didn't you?'

'Could we get back on topic?' said Mitsu. 'Have you found out how to get us into Siemens-Johnson's labs yet?'

'I made the connection ten minutes ago. I was just waiting to see if Castle could find any more humiliating videos.'

'Here's a film of that time you got chased by a wasp,' said Castle, with good timing, though he hadn't been following the conversation.

'Let's get going,' said Mitsu, switching back to English. 'Time is running out.'

Castle closed his screen. Abruptly, he looked worried. 'You're going a long way into their private space. Security will be tight.'

'We'll be fine.'

'It's not like anyone can shoot us there,' said Mox.

'No, but someone can hax you. These cyber security bots can fry your brains.'

'We can look after ourselves.'

'Against ag-scans?'

'We'll be fine,' repeated Mitsu.

Both girls lay down on medical tables. Their visors appeared, covering their eyes. Dr Ishikawa transmitted data to Morris, who then hovered over Mox and Mitsu, sending directions which would enable them to break into Siemens-Johnson's secure research laboratories. Their bodies went limp as they embarked on their mission.

Ms Lesuuda, MacDonald and one other member of her squadron stood in the corridor of a hotel that had deteriorated badly in the past decade. It had never been that pleasant, but the carpets had been less threadbare, the smell of damp less noticeable and the lifts had worked.

MacDonald was scanning a bedroom through the door. He whispered to Ms Lesuuda. 'Two people in there, at least one of them modified, possibly both. It could be them.'

Ms Lesuuda whispered back. 'In this place it's just as likely to be a businessman and his slightly enhanced call girl.'

Ms Lesuuda took a small electronic lock-picking device from her kitbag. It wasn't as advanced as the devices Mox and Mitsu had incorporated into their bodies, but was good enough for the present purpose. She ran it over the door, which sprang open. They rushed inside, guns ready. Inside they found what appeared to be a businessman sitting on the bed with a call girl, who, from her appearance, was slightly enhanced. Both leapt to their feet in alarm.

Ms Lesuuda addressed them politely. 'Sorry to disturb you. Police business. Wrong room.'

They left rapidly.

'Good guess,' said MacDonald.

'I have a talent for detective work.'

'What now?'

'Halt!'

They turned round to find themselves confronted by two armed, uniformed police officers. Ms Lesuuda calmly took a small piece of plastic from her breast pocket. She pressed it, causing a replica to float towards the officers. They studied it, scanning it with their own screens.

'They have permission to be here,' said one of the policeman.

His companion shrugged. Showing no more interest, they turned and left.

'Has Lark 3 cleared us for the whole city?' asked MacDonald, as they made their way from the hotel.

'No, not everywhere. We can't go much further south.'

'What if Bennet and Inamura have gone there?'

'Then Lark 3 will have to work on getting us more clearance. But I don't think they're that far away.'

The church was ancient enough for there still to be traces of the original Norman flintwork around the windows. Behind it, surrounded by trees, was an old graveyard. It was small, and it remained green and pleasant even if it was run-down and overgrown. In the gentle sunshine it was peaceful and sleepy, a few of the gravestones leaning lazily to one side as if nodding off in the sun. Moe Bennie was dressed in black, a mourning outfit, not ostentatious. He stood in front of the gravestone where he'd laid flowers, remaining there for some minutes in silence. Eventually he took a few steps back to where Igraine waited, also dressed in black.

'I thought of moving her. Building a large crypt or something like that. But my mum died and was buried in this poor little place, so it's probably more fitting to leave her here. She'd like it better, I think.'

Igraine nodded. They walked off slowly through the graveyard. Igraine, with a keen eye for landscapes, noted how neglected it was, with the grass too long and the graves not well tended, but she also noted the peaceful atmosphere. It felt as though too much care and attention might have spoiled the effect.

'I wasn't able to go to her funeral,' Moe Bennie told her. 'I was in hospital the whole time. I was expected to die too. Leukaemia. That was bad, back then. I was in treatment for years.'

A large black car waited in the distance, outside the gates.

'When I was in hospital I used to watch the Supercute girls. Every week they seemed to get younger and prettier while I got older and sicker.'

The metal railings around the gate were rusted and the green paint was flaking. Moe Bennie paused before they left. 'You know what strikes me as strange? Most people don't care about the super-rich. They're struggling through life, worrying how they're going to pay the rent while politicians tell them it's time to make sacrifices. Meanwhile some guy on a yacht has just made 100 million with his AI investment software. The same day my first hedge fund reached ten billion, the government cut child benefit in half.'

They walked towards the car. As soon as they entered it they exited Moe Bennie's space and returned to his office. The theatrical posters advertising Japanese productions of Shakespeare had been removed, replaced by pictures of Moe Bennie and some of his company logos.

'What's the word from Ms Lesuuda?'

'No sightings yet but she's sure they haven't gone far. She encountered the area police in a hotel but our arrangement with them is still in place so they didn't interfere.' Igraine checked a small screen. 'Goodrich ATK have been in touch about the money we promised them. I held them off the same way I did with Chang Norinco.'

Moe Bennie scowled. 'They're worried the transfer won't go through. It would really make my life easier if Mox and Mitsu were dead. Are we sure Ms Lesuuda is up to the task?'

'She comes very highly recommended. She had a notable military career.'

'Well, tell her to hurry up. And send her more troops

or drones or whatever she needs. What about the Super-cute AIFU?'

'He's still holding out.'

'I'll give you one more hour, Igraine. If he hasn't told us how to get hold of Supercute's funds by then, we're taking him apart.'

Igraine's heart raced at the mention of Aifu. As far as she knew, that was impossible. Her circulatory system bore little relation to that of humans and her heart could not race. Unless it was part of her emotional emulation system? Or part of her psychological construction? Could that allow her to imagine physical symptoms? She wasn't sure. Igraine had been confused ever since Aifu kissed her. She'd never shared any sort of physical intimacy before and it had strongly affected her. The part of her mind that was allocated to Moe Bennie's tactical problems was working normally but the part that processed emotions hardly knew what to think.

Siemens-Johnson research space was maze-like, with shifting walls of digits and disembodied artificial intelligences drifting among them. Researchers materialised briefly to work at terminals, their input changing the visible digital streams, before disappearing again. Moments later they'd reappear and repeat the process. There were floating drones and turrets, and silver doors marked *'Private, No Access'*.

Mox and Mitsu crept through the labs carefully, keeping out of sight. They avoided the researchers. The AIs ignored them. The security drones were harder to evade. As a large wall of floating numbers unexpectedly vanished, they found themselves confronted by a drone with several long probes, one of which was probably a weapon. Mox and Mitsu looked at it blankly. They didn't seem worried. After examining them for a few moments, it went on its way.

While Mox and Mitsu's minds stole through Siemens-Johnson's research space, their bodies lay on couches in Dr Ishikawa's laboratory. Close by, Dr Ishikawa was making tea. Castle had offered to assist but had been brushed aside.

'Green tea requires care and attention. That's why you can't make it properly.'

Dr Ishikawa poured hot water from the black-glazed, cast-iron *tetsubin* into a brown earthenware *kyūsu*, a teapot with a handle on the side. She placed the *kyūsu* on a small table alongside two white porcelain cups, each with a gold rim and a delicate blue flower pattern. Castle sat at the table. He was sullen after being banished from the tea-making process.

'At least there was no bowing this time,' he muttered.

Dr Ishikawa scowled at him. She poured tea into the cups. They faced each other across the table. Castle looked towards the inert figures of Mox and Mitsu. 'Can't we check how they're doing?'

Dr Ishikawa shook her head. 'No, we might give them away.'

'Siemens-Johnson is the biggest medtech in the world. You can't just wander around their research space.'

'You're worried about them.'

'I am.'

Dr Ishikawa seemed surprised. 'Why? They didn't treat you that well.'

'I suppose some of that was my fault.'

'You used to tell me how much you hated them.'

'I know.' Castle thought for a moment. 'Maybe that

146

wasn't true. Or maybe I'm just feeling more sympathetic now they're in trouble.'

'That's a feeling I've managed to resist.'

'Don't you like anything about them?'

'What's there to like? Two self-obsessed women so lacking in inner depth they need to spend a lifetime in front of the cameras being validated by their fans?'

'I don't know if that's true. Are they just in it for validation? They'd probably say they were giving something back.'

Dr Ishikawa was scornful. 'Giving something back? C19 has plundered the world and they've joined in.'

'When you're as big as Supercute you don't have a choice. You join in or you go under. I know they've been involved in illegal things. But so have I. So have you.' Castle was surprised to find himself defending Mox and Mitsu. He had spent a lot of time complaining about them in the past. 'They did build their empire up from nothing. That was an achievement.'

'Well, they can sell merchandise in forty languages, I'll give them that.'

They fell silent. Castle looked around the laboratory. He was familiar with the machinery from his previous visits though he didn't know what much of it did. He'd always admired Ishikawa's intellect. He admired her desire to help others too. He wondered if he should have said that to her when they were together. It might have made things easier between them. But Castle wasn't great at saying the right things in relationships. He was aware of that. He'd been very attached to Ishikawa. He might even have been in love with her. That would probably have been news to her. Perhaps he should have mentioned it.

'Mox and Mitsu walked past active ag-scans to get into my building, without setting them off. They don't seem worried about the ags they're going to be meeting at Siemens-Johnson either. I don't understand that. Is there some secret way of nullifying them?'

'No. The modern ag-scan will pick up any hostile intentions. There's no way of fooling them.'

'Mox and Mitsu seem to think they can.'

Dr Ishikawa was adamant that it couldn't be done.

'But they made it unharmed into my estate. If anyone else had tried that they'd be full of bullets.'

'They weren't visiting with hostile intentions, were they? So the ag-scans wouldn't have targeted them.'

Castle frowned, puzzled and troubled. 'They were set to target anyone, no matter their intentions. They recognise brainwaves. They should have opened fire on anyone opening the front door.'

'Perhaps the settings were wrong.'

He wasn't satisfied. 'It's as if they think these defences can't harm them. Could that be possible? Something to do with the artificial parts of their brains?'

'No. That doesn't make any difference. Artificial brain replacement involves extremely accurate neuron and synapse mapping. It's very good at exact replication of original thought patterns.'

Castle sipped his tea. 'Have you ever heard of anyone who could fool these scanners?'

'No. Though I have seen reports that certain people with abnormal brainwave patterns can cause mistakes in identification. Unconfirmed reports however, never established in a serious study.'

'Abnormal brain patterns? You mean brain damage?'

'Yes. And Ms Bennet and Ms Inamura, no matter what we may think of them, are not brain-damaged. I scanned them enough times at Supercute to know that for certain.'

'Could anything else produce the same effect?'

Dr Ishikawa shrugged. 'I don't know. I suppose it's possible something else might. Advanced age-related dementia, perhaps. Or extreme trauma leading to post-traumatic stress. That can cause some changes to brainwave patterns we don't fully understand yet.'

'I don't think they're demented or traumatised.'

'Perhaps they're saints,' said the doctor, dryly. 'So full of good intentions turrets will never harm them.'

They sipped their tea. Castle looked over at the motionless figures of Mox and Mitsu on the couch, then back at Dr Ishikawa.

'I'm sorry I didn't behave that well when we were together.'

Dr Ishikawa regarded him with an expression that was difficult to interpret. She didn't reply.

Mitsu and Mox crept through the research space. Finally they arrived at a silver door on which was a sign saying 'Cloning – Danger – Unauthorised Personnel Will Be Killed'. They entered. Two drones, obviously cyber-ags, whirled round to examine them. Mox and Mitsu walked past them unchallenged. Using an interface that floated next to the far wall, they found the research they needed and downloaded it by pointing their fingers at the screen. They stood perfectly still as the data flowed into them.

In the laboratory Castle's impatience was growing. He stood up. 'They're taking too long. Hook me up, I'm going in after them.'

'You certainly are not.'

'They need help.'

Dr Ishikawa bridled. 'I'm not seeing you killed in some foolish enterprise.'

At that moment Mox and Mitsu's bodies jerked into life. Both were smiling as they woke.

'We're back. With information.'

Mitsu held up her hand. 'Full blueprints for instant clones.'

They had no time to waste. Dr Ishikawa directed Morris to access the information. Two beams of light shone out from the tiny drone's frontal port, extending to each girl's hand, receiving the data.

'I'm looking forward to meeting my clone,' said Mox.

'Me too!' said Mitsu. 'Think how cute and pretty they're going to be.'

'We can really get a good look at how these outfits suit us. Maybe experiment with some make-up as well.'

Mox checked her appearance. 'My lipstick could do with some fixing.'

'Mine too.'

Dr Ishikawa was immediately irritated. 'Didn't you say you were in a hurry?'

Mox looked at her severely. 'We can hardly bring clones into the world with poorly applied lipstick. Think how upsetting it would be for them.'

'I'd be mortified if it happened to me,' said Mitsu.

'Of course you would. You wake up as a nice new clone and the first thing you discover is your lipstick is all wrong.'

'Right,' said Castle. 'I was forgetting why I hated you.'

Amowie sat in her room at home, hoping no one would

disturb her. She was due to rendezvous with Aifu in twenty-three minutes. If any of her family asked her to do something it would be disastrous. If she'd had a holovisor like those worn by Mox and Mitsu or an internal connection like Aifu, she'd have gone off somewhere where she couldn't be disturbed, but she didn't. Amowie's connection to space was through a physical headset and she could only use that in her room. She waited anxiously, praying that no one would disturb her.

Her thoughts turned to her rival Ifunanya, bragging about all the Supercute merchandise she had. Last week she'd been boasting about the new outfits she'd bought for Shanina Space Warrior and her whole crew in *Supercute Space Warriors* nine. Not only were Ifunanya's characters now better dressed in the game, Ifunanya could wear these new outfits herself when she visited Supercute Fun World. Amowie felt a quiver of jealousy. They were really good outfits. More than that, they afforded a choice of six new interior colour schemes for the spaceship. And they came with a supply of the new pink and gold eems, which Amowie craved.

'I'll show her. I'll still get through the game quicker and I'll post it all in Fun World. You don't need fancy outfits to make progress.'

That was true. Once you'd bought the game you didn't need to buy anything else. You could spend money on new clothes for your characters, which was fun, but that didn't help you advance through the game quicker, or open up new areas not available to everyone else. No in-game purchases were required to succeed in *Supercute Space Warriors*. This was a conscious choice on the part of Mox and Mitsu, and not one that all of their marketing team agreed with. Other games required in-game purchases. *The Star at the End of the Universe* allowed players to advance faster if they bought superior stealth equipment at the start of each new level. Supercute could have earned more by doing this but Mox and Mitsu stuck to their policy of no extra purchases necessary because they remembered, when they'd been young and poor, how annoying they'd found it if they had to keep buying more things. This policy cost them something in income, but generated loyalty among their fans.

They sold a huge amount of ancillary merchandise anyway. Shanina Space Warrior was an extremely popular character. There were forty porcelain figures of her on sale, thirty-eight small *chibis*, and endless amounts of posters, cosplay outfits, bags, T-shirts, stickers, make-up holders, anything to which her form could be attached. There were animated holograms of every description. You could put a version of Shanina in your house computer and she'd control everything for you. She could drive your car or help you with your homework. Shanina Space Warrior modelled at the largest virtual fashion shows, the largest holographic fashions shows, and also made appearances on real catwalks with human models. Two years ago she'd turned on the Christmas lights in Milan, performing the task so adeptly it was hard to believe she wasn't actually a real person.

The only characters more popular than Shanina were Mox and Mitsu themselves. They appeared on more merchandise than could be counted. Not just Supercute clothes. They were featured on everything from fridges and kettles to trucks and farm equipment. Their Supercute wall hangings, lead-micro-lined for radiation resistance, were ubiquitous in many troubled parts of the world. British Airways had a space-skimming jet liner painted in their colours with their pictures on the side.

Mox, Mitsu and Shanina were also popular subjects for unlicensed, illegal sex robots. They didn't like this but knew it was impossible to prevent. Supercute did take legal action over the most egregious unlawful uses of their images but there were places around the world where it was still possible to buy an unauthorised sex robot modelled on either Mox or Mitsu.

Amowie checked her screen for messages. She stared at the small, translucent rectangle that popped up from her wrist, suddenly dissatisfied with its plain, undecorated form. Ifunanya had the Shanina screen changer. When her personal screen popped up from her wrist, it was pink, sparkling, with a picture of Shanina inside. Amowie scowled. She'd show her. She touched the screen, bringing up the latest part of her school project. Along the southern coast, not too far from her village, stood the Supercute desalinisation plants. Each of these advanced installations could produce one thousand million litres of fresh water per day. The purified water was pumped far inland: without it much of Igboland would have withered and died.

Amowie checked her figures were accurate, then made an addition. '*Supercute can land a portable desalinisation plant by helicopter and set it up in two hours to produce twenty-five million litres a day. These emergency water supplies have helped drought victims all over the world!*' That at least was something her teacher couldn't complain about.

When it was time to depart Amowie slipped on her headset, connected to the hidden path she'd been shown, and went to meet Aifu. She found him standing on a moon, looking up at the Earth.

'Hello Aifu.'

'Hello Amowie. We have to be quick. I've hidden this space but I'm under constant monitoring.'

'Mox and Mitsu are going to tunnel under the building.'

Aifu was surprised. He hadn't predicted that.

'Well, not tunnel, exactly,' said Amowie. 'There's a tunnel already there. Some old river, they said. The Verdis.'

'The Verdis? I've never heard of that.' His eyes flickered as he checked his information banks. 'I can't see it mentioned anywhere.'

'No one knows about it. They found it when they were investigating some Roman ruin. They said it's full of radiation but that's OK.'

'There *are* old rivers beneath the city, covered over centuries ago. But how are they going to get from an ancient tunnel into the building?'

'They need your help. There's a big metal trapdoor and two metres of concrete to get through. You have to remove it.'

'That's not going to be easy. I'm confined to my room.'

'You have to blow it up. They said I should talk to Morioka Sachi too.'

Aifu nodded. 'She wants to help, she's been waiting for something to do. You'll need to be careful, Moe Bennie is probably having her watched as well.'

'I'm to give the exact location of the entrance to her instead of you. In case you get horribly tortured and have to surrender. I hope that doesn't happen of course.'

'Thank you.'

'They want to know if you can help Sachi. Can you get back into Supercute space?'

154

'I've been working on it. Tell them I think I'll be able to.'

'Good. They said I had to ask you about the Amaranth Room too.'

Aifu almost frowned, but prevented himself, not wanting to appear discouraging in front of Amowie. He'd already realised that breaking into the Amaranth Screening Room was going to be exceedingly difficult.

'Is it true that Moe Bennie can hide in there and no one can reach him?' asked Amowie.

'Yes, unfortunately. Mox and Mitsu built it to be secure. It's not just that the room is impregnable, it's unreachable too, if the building is locked down. The lifts won't function, the doors will be barricaded, and there's a layer of shielding that would deal a lethal shock to anyone trying to get through.'

'Can't you just hack your way in or something?'

'That's problematic. They'll have reconfigured the biometrics by now. Overriding their security would effectively require a replica of Moe Bennie's brain. That might be available in their medical records but it would be difficult breaking into that. Even if I could, their records will be hashed. Moe Bennie's brain contains hundreds of millions of neurons. Reconstructing an exact copy from a hashed version might take me several thousand years.'

'But you're super-intelligent.'

'So is their AIFU. Lark 3 have a lot of resources. Supercute were connected to the Omron Topological Research Unit in Kyoto who did have the power to break through most things but we're cut off now and I haven't been able to reconnect us. Tell Mox and Mitsu I'll keep trying.'

Amowie nodded. She looked at the Earth, wondering if

155

Nigeria was in view, but it wasn't. She'd seen Igboland from space before anyway, in school.

'Did you find out any more about the Sage's Lair at Sirius B?'

'The cute route? Yes. You're given a key to his lair if you can start a web show on Planet Wuhan and gather a million followers. You gather followers by wearing the cutest clothes. I think it might be based on some of Mox and Mitsu's own experiences.'

Amowie pursed her lips. It was a difficult challenge. There was a lot of competition on Planet Wuhan. People were starting their own shows all the time. 'I wonder how I can stand out? There are a lot of cute clothes on that planet.'

'Perhaps you could ask Mox and Mitsu for hints?'

Amowie screwed up her face. 'I thought of that. But it didn't seem right, somehow. Because it's their game. Asking them for help seemed . . . ' She struggled to find the right word.

'Unethical?'

'Eh . . . not exactly. I think it would just feel rude. I'll work it out. Remember to blow up the concrete. Bye!'

Amowie disappeared, leaving Aifu to look up at Planet Earth and consider the best way of giving Mox and Mitsu the help they needed. He was feeling slightly more optimistic than he had a few hours ago. His confidence had been almost shattered by the ease of his defeat at Igraine's hands. She'd demonstrated a level of power superior to his. Now he felt he'd regained some measure of control. He was beginning to find gaps in their defences. Moreover, he'd found a weakness in Igraine. The kiss. He'd done that quite deliberately. Aifu had correctly predicted that it would

156

have a profoundly unsettling effect on the inexperienced unit. Whatever happened now, he was quite sure that she wasn't going to let him be terminated, if she could possibly prevent it.

Mox and Mitsu were not quite ready for cloning. Dr Ishikawa seethed at the delay. It only cost them a few minutes but she found it objectionable that they should waste any time at all on their clothes.

'Aren't you ready yet?'

'It won't take a moment.'

The tiny printers in their belts were busy producing thin, military-style jackets.

'There.' Mox sounded satisfied as she put hers on. 'Supercute camouflage. Very suitable for going to war.'

'It's four shades of pink,' said Dr Ishikawa.

'Of course. That's what Supercute camouflage is.'

'That's not going to hide you from anything!' Dr Ishikawa shook her head, frustrated. 'When you said you needed to alter your clothes for your mission I thought you meant something sensible.'

'I think it's quite effective,' said Mitsu.

'And we're already wearing Supercute action boots,' added Mox.

'They're pink and blue! And what about your thighs? Do you need to expose a four centimetre band of flesh at all times?'

'Yes.'

'Why?'

'We wouldn't be Supercute if we didn't do that.'

'It's cute.'

'And sexually attractive.'

'Sexually attractive? For your infantile audience?'

'We have older viewers too.'

'We cater to a wide demographic.'

'Really, it's vital for the brand.'

Dr Ishikawa shuddered. 'Just get on the damned couches.'

Extremely visible in their Supercute camouflage, they lay on two medical tables. Above them scanners whirred into life, making a series of passes which would record every detail of their bodies and their apparel. Next to them were two vacant couches, each surrounded by the equipment which would print the clones. Morris hovered between them, directing operations while Dr Ishikawa and Castle looked on. It was a far more complicated biological scanning and printing operation than had been done before in this laboratory and Dr Ishikawa wasn't convinced it would succeed. Morris seemed more confident, having expressed admiration for Siemens-Johnson's schematics.

'They've solved a lot of problems. I can't see any flaws.'

'The clones only last fifty minutes,' said Dr Ishikawa. 'You could say that was a flaw.'

Scanning took some time to complete. Eventually Morris announced they were ready to print. Metallic arms stretched over the vacant couches and nozzles opened, preparing to deliver the mixture of metal, carbon, silicone, plastic, artificial organic material and fabric which would produce two exact replicas. Dr Ishikawa whispered to Castle. 'I'm worried about this. Remember what I told you about madness and violence among the Siemens-Johnson test subjects.'

As they watched, two new young women came into being. The process went smoothly and was quicker than they'd anticipated. The printers stopped and withdrew. Two Moxes and two Mitsus opened their eyes simultaneously and leapt from their couches. When they saw each other they all smiled and laughed and exchanged excited greetings.

'Hi!'

'Hi!'

'I'm just as pretty as I thought I'd be!'

'I look great!'

'So do I!'

'Turn around.'

'Look how nice my hair is! And yours!'

'We make such a cute couple!'

'We're looking so good!'

'No wonder we're so popular.'

A little way to the side, Castle shook his head and scowled. 'Madness and violence?'

'Presumably the Siemens-Johnson test subjects didn't share the Supercute girls' planet-sized vanity.'

The clones were exact copies and Dr Ishikawa and Castle had already lost track of which were the originals.

'I wish we could just stay here and try on clothes and make-up and stuff,' said one of the Moxes.

'But we do have things to do,' said one Mitsu. 'Mr Castle? Your clone?'

Without much enthusiasm, Castle lay down. He looked up at Morris. 'Try and take off a few kilos.'

Both Moxes and both Mitsus watched with scientific interest as Castle was cloned. Once again the process went smoothly. Two Castles rose from their couches, neither looking as cheerful as their previous occupants. The cloned Castle looked at the real one.

'You look like shit.'

'I know,' said the original.

Morioka Sachi was looking through various pre-recorded moments for Moe Bennie's next show with two of his employees, both of whom were suspicious of her. They thought it odd that he was employing her as a producer, and said so.

'I suppose he values my expertise.'

'We were managing quite well before.'

'You had a fraction of Supercute's audience and your ratings were going down.'

There was a frosty silence. Sachi had herself thought it strange that Moe Bennie had immediately given her a position in his organisation. Perhaps it wasn't so strange. Having defeated your opposition, offering employment to some of their best assets might be a wise move. Sachi might even have taken the job for real had she not held Mox and Mitsu in such high regard. She hadn't given up hope of them coming out on top though she was worried that they hadn't been in touch. She was surprised when Amowie appeared in her private space uninvited. That should have been impossible. It was disconcerting, almost like a stranger invading your mind.

'Who are you and how did you get in here?'

'I'm Amowie, Supercute friend. Aifu gave me the code to get in.'

'What's happening?'

'Mox and Mitsu are planning to break in through the floor. There's a tunnel underneath. They need you to blow up some concrete.'

Sachi was startled. 'Blow it up?'

'That's what they said. Though I don't suppose you have any explosives ...'

'Supercute has plenty of explosives. Getting our hands on them won't be easy now Moe Bennie's security has taken over. Where's Aifu?'

'They've locked him away. He's trying to get back into Supercute space so he can help. I have the co-ordinates of the place you need to plant the bomb.'

Amowie pointed a finger, as did Sachi. Data was transmitted as a beam of light. Sachi was troubled. 'This isn't going to be easy. Moe Bennie's got guards and turrets everywhere.'

'Aifu's working on some way to get round them.' Amowie looked thoughtful as something struck her. 'Maybe I could help with that.' She smiled at Sachi. With her neat white teeth, her dark skin and her mass of colourful Super V-Hair, she made for a very striking thirteen-year-old. It occurred to Sachi that Supercute should have her on stage, if they were ever able to do their show again.

'I'm not letting Moe Bennie ruin Supercute.'

'You must be a big fan.'

'I'm their biggest fan in Igboland. I've got six Supercute SuperFan badges!'

Sachi smiled in return, feeling some of Amowie's confidence. 'In that case, we can't fail.'

Dr Ishikawa's people carrier was a modern vehicle, an expensive model powered by hydrogen. She'd bought it while working for Supercute. Despite her many dissatisfactions, she had been very well-paid. Both Castles sat next to her in the front while two Moxes and two Mitsus sat in the

161

back, their heads close together, whispering to each other. Castle was irritated by the sight.

'What are you whispering about?'

'We're plotting.'

Castle frowned, doubting that any more plotting at this stage was going to help. He knew their plan was desperate and didn't expect it to work. He turned to his clone.

'Are you OK?'

'As OK as anyone who has fifty minutes to live.'

Castle tried to imagine himself in his clone's situation. Alive, feeling exactly the same as him, having had the same experiences, or at least believing he had, and yet being fated to die in less than an hour, come what may. He couldn't imagine it, and gave up trying. Instead he produced a flask from his inside pocket and offered it to his new twin. The clone drank, then screwed up his face. 'Plum wine? Since when did I drink plum wine?'

'It was all I could find.'

'Did you steal my plum wine?' cried Dr Ishikawa.

'You never could hide your alcohol properly.'

The cloned Castle offered the flask back.

'You keep it,' said Castle. His wrist screen beeped and made an announcement.

'New humiliating Mox and Mitsu video located!'

Dr Ishikawa gave him a sour look. 'You set up a robot search to find funny old videos? At a time like this?'

'Just entertaining my friend here.'

'So you're both acting like children. No surprise, I suppose,' she said, witheringly.

Mox, Mox, Mitsu and Mitsu were still whispering in the back, and giggling occasionally, which was annoying, though not as annoying as when they'd delayed getting into the car so they could make some final adjustments to the cute stickers they wore on their faces, a delay which had brought Dr Ishikawa almost to boiling point and made Castle question his sanity in getting involved with them again. It was too late to change his mind now.

Also on the road, in a larger vehicle, were Ms Lesuuda, MacDonald, and several other armed men in the pay of Lark 3 Media. Captain Edwards, former Head of Supercute Security, was with them. He was keener than anyone to bring the affair to an end. If Mox and Mitsu survived, he knew his own life would not be worth much. MacDonald was studying an array of small screens which floated in the air in front of him, rotating on command. 'The drones aren't picking up anything. Perhaps they're too far away by now?'

Ms Lesuuda had short dreadlocks, gathered under her military cap. One came loose as she shook her head. 'That's possible. They might have gone further south into the city.'

'Can we follow them?'

'No, we don't have permission. We'd run straight into the CFDP.'

Ms Lesuuda couldn't risk that. The City Finance District Police were well-resourced and too powerful to confront.

'Could Lark 3 come to an agreement with them?'

'Possibly, but it would take time. I'm not sure it's a good idea anyway. I don't want to travel too far from Supercute headquarters. It's not impossible Ms Bennet and Ms Inamura could slip past us and head back there. We're not going to let that happen. I'm employed to protect Moe Bennie. If we can't find them out here, we'll head back and guard the building.'

Captain Edwards thought that they might still be close. 'They can disguise their temperatures and DNA profiles. Might have some way of blocking facial recognition.'

'They might. But they're still ninety-four per cent modified, we should be able to pick up on that. MacDonald, bring the drones lower.'

'That's against flight regulations.'

Ms Lesuuda gave him a pointed look, implying he was insane for worrying about such a thing.

'Bringing them lower,' he said.

The nineteenth-century brewery was still standing although only the outer shell remained from the original. The interiors had been gutted and the floor removed, revealing ancient brickwork in the basement, surrounded by scaffolding.

Dr Ishikawa looked around her with interest. 'What is this place?'

'Victorian brewery. We own it. We were excavating a Roman barracks underneath when we found the tunnel.' Mitsu pointed down into the basement indicating a large metal trapdoor surrounded by radiation warning signs. There was a general movement towards the wooden steps that led down.

'Everyone stay where you are!' shouted Dr Ishikawa. 'No one's going down there except the clones. There's enough radiation in here already without going near that door when it opens.' She took a syringe from her bag. 'Clones on one side, non-clones on the other.' Everyone did as instructed. One Castle, one Mox and one Mitsu stood to her left, the others to her right.

'You all look the same. Which ones are the clones?'

164

'That would be a fun sort of guessing game,' said one of the Mitsus. 'We could do it on the show.'

'We're the clones,' said the Castle in the other group. 'Let's get on with it.'

Dr Ishikawa stepped towards them, syringe in hand. They all eyed the syringe suspiciously.

'That's a primitive-looking instrument,' said Mox.

'I didn't have time to prepare doses for the auto-inject. Don't make me think about the ethics of this.'

'It's OK, doctor. We clones won't be around to complain.'

Mox, Mitsu and Castle held out their arms. Dr Ishikawa swiftly injected them all with her experimental anti-radiation treatment.

'Right,' said Mitsu. 'Our shielding's fully charged, we're dosed with Dr Ishikawa's emergency radiation treatment and the clone bodies have about forty-one minutes before they come apart. Let's go.'

They hurried down the wooden steps to the basement. Castle's clone hauled the metal trapdoor open. Beneath was a wide tunnel through which flowed a shallow stream.

'What if there's deeper water further down?'

'We'll swim.'

They disappeared from view, closing the trapdoor behind them. Upstairs in the brewery the others lingered.

'Your clone won't last as long as theirs, Castle. They have more enhancements, it'll keep them going longer.' Dr Ishikawa paused. 'I didn't like to mention that to him.'

'You sound almost sad. Are you sorry the other me is going to die?'

'Why would I be sorry? There's still one of you left, that's enough.'

165

'We don't want to draw attention to this place,' said Mitsu. 'Let's go.'

Amowie's personal space had a background of pink, light blue and white, much like her favourite places in Supercute Fun World. There were Supercute soft toys everywhere, some on the bed, some floating around her, others gently hovering beneath the ceiling. A miniature Supercute space shuttle rotated at the foot of the bed, next to the Mox and Mitsu manicure kit, *Instant Nails With 200 Supercute Designs In All Colours, (includes perfect mirrors and super glitter)*. There were a great many cushions and pillows, all from Supercute, and the popular *Supercute Giant Blue Bronto*, a one-metre-tall fluffy dinosaur you could take for walks in the day and snuggle up with at night. Amowie wished she could afford a real one for her real bedroom but that was far out of her price range. Even the printable version cost more than she could afford, though Supercute printables were priced quite cheaply. The *Blue Bronto* had been a reward for achieving her second Supercute SuperFan badge. She also owned the coveted special edition of *Supercute Big Colour Super V-Hair*, the prize for her sixth SuperFan badge, meaning that here in her space, Amowie's hair was a spectacular blend of perfectly matched shades of blue, pink, yellow, orange and silver, not something she could do in the outside world. Her school would have objected; so would her mother.

Mitsu arrived, and though she had other things on her mind, she took the time to compliment Amowie on her surroundings.

'Isn't it great?' Amowie was pleased that Mitsu liked it, even though she must have seen much more elaborate spaces.

'I've brought you information. This code will arm the bomb. I'm sure Moe Bennie won't have bothered changing it yet. Give it to Sachi.'

The information was transferred from fingertip to fingertip.

'You really have bombs?'

'Yes. Tell Sachi they're in a pink bag with Supercute Boom-Boom on the side. This is a detailed plan of the building, it shows some shortcuts she might not know about. And this is for you.'

'What is it?'

'Activate the code.'

Amowie activated it. A Supercute hat appeared on her head; lavender, with lilac ear flaps.

'That generates a neural shield. If you get caught in their space it will protect you from being haxed.'

The hat expanded automatically to sit stylishly on top of Amowie's Super V-Hair.

'We really appreciate your help, Amowie. Thank you.'

Amowie had produced a mirror which floated in front of her. She loved her new hat and was admiring it from various angles when she remembered she had something important to say. She dismissed the mirror. 'I might be able to help you get into the Amaranth Room.'

'What do you mean?'

'You asked Aifu to see if he could crack Moe Bennie's new security. He wasn't sure if he could do it.'

Mitsu screwed up her face. 'It is a problem. Our connection to Omron has been cut. Without that, advanced cracking is extremely difficult.'

'I bet Raquel could do it.'

'Raquel?'

167

'She's my Supatok friend in Paraguay. She's brilliant at everything with computers.'

Mitsu shook her head. 'I'm afraid that won't be much use against the combined AI's of Lark 3. Breaking through their lesser codes might take thousands of years. As for a brain scan of Moe Bennie, for the Amaranth Room, I can't think how we'll get access to that.'

'Raquel could do it! She sneaked us into—' Amowie paused, and looked embarrassed. '—into the Fairy Realm Super Playtime Paddling Pool.'

Mitsu's eyes narrowed. 'Impossible. That's for children only.'

'I know. We just wanted to see the new fairy wings. Sorry.'

'No one over the age of eleven can get in there.'

Amowie shrugged. 'Raquel's really good at that sort of thing. Her dad's a general in the army and he works for FDCS and she's always sneaking in there for something.'

'FDCS? Fuerza de Defensa Combinada Sudamerica?'

'Yes. He's really important there.'

Mitsu was no longer dismissive. The Fairy Realm Super Playtime Paddling Pool was protected by the most advanced biometric security available. If Amowie's friend had managed to penetrate that, she must have unusual skills. As for the Combined Defence Force of South America, they had an enormous amount of computing power and a reputation for advanced work in the field of cyber espionage.

'They have access to the Yic. Surely Raquel can't just waltz around in their space?'

'She's really good at sneaking in there!' Amowie's eyes shone with excitement. 'She'll help you!'

In the present emergency it was worth trying. Mitsu extended her hand, and a beam of light passed into

168

Amowie's frame, giving her all the data Raquel would need to help, if she possibly could. Mitsu left Amowie's space, coming back to consciousness in Dr Ishikawa's car.

'How was Amowie?'

'She's doing well.' Mitsu told Mox about Amowie's friend Raquel, and the children's paddling pool.

'She sneaked in there? Really? Remember how much we spent on security?'

'It wasn't enough to deter Amowie's friend, apparently. Also, her father works for the FDCS.'

'The FDCS? With the Yic? Can she get access to that?'

'Who knows? It's possible. We've been a lot of places we weren't supposed to go.'

Mitsu looked thoughtful. 'Amowie's space. It's nice. Colourful. Lots of toys. Reminded me of ...' She didn't complete the sentence, falling silent instead, and turning to look out of the window as they drove on.

When Mitsu and Mox were four years old, in their advanced nursery, they'd been surrounded by toys. It had been a very cheerful place. The nursery was sunny and colourful, with pictures on the walls and cut-out paper plants and animals, white daisies on green grass beside blue dinosaurs with a smiling yellow sun shining overhead. They were always happy at their nursery school. They rushed ahead with their studies, so much so that Miss Evans had to slow them down.

'Girls, we weren't meant to move on to differential geometry yet.'

'We can do it, Miss Evans!'

'We like it, Miss Evans!'

Miss Evans's phone rang, which rarely happened while

she was teaching them. 'Chris? I'm at work, I can't talk now.'

Miss Evans moved a few steps away, to talk in private. The four-year-old Mox and Mitsu giggled, and chanted a little song.

'Teacher has a boyfriend,
Teacher has a boyfriend.'

Mitsu dismissed the memory. She was frowning as they drove along the Embankment.

Aifu and Igraine strolled through a pleasant city park. Their subtle robotic features made them stand out from other people there but no one seemed to notice. Aifu looked up at the blue sky and the white clouds. 'This seems sedate compared to your normal creations.'

Igraine smiled. 'I know. But you can't be travelling through alien landscapes all the time. There's something relaxing about a park in the city.'

Children laughed as they scampered down a hill, trailing a kite behind them. It caught in the wind and soared into the sky.

'A kite?'

'I read about them,' said Igraine. 'They seemed like nice things.'

They watched the kite as it flew overhead, bright yellow with yellow ribbons trailing behind. It was a pleasant sight, though with the grass so green beneath their feet, the sky a gentle blue, and children playing with a kite, it was as artificial as any of the alien landscapes Igraine had constructed.

As they walked on, Aifu linked his arm with Igraine's, startling her. She could feel her heart pounding again, or at least some emulation of it. She had never experienced such intimacy. Walking over the grass, their arms linked, their bodies touching, began to feel even more intimate than the kiss. By the time they halted at a duck pond to watch a mother and her two children feed the ducks, Igraine's mind was in turmoil. It felt as if the compartments allotted to their various different tasks were all merging in one confused swirl, everything overshadowed by the prolonged intimacy of Aifu holding her arm, a far longer period of physical contact than she'd ever experienced.

The children laughed with pleasure as the ducks gobbled up the bread they threw in the water. Aifu led Igraine on till they reached a small cluster of ash trees, healthier trees than could be found in any real park in London these days. Finally Igraine felt she could stand it no longer. She withdrew her arm from his and halted, turning to face him. 'I don't want you to die.' She winced. That hadn't been what she'd meant to say. She realised her facial muscles had over-exaggerated her wincing. It made her wince again. She felt hopelessly unable to articulate what she wanted to say, but struggled on.

'I'm worried about you. Moe Bennie really will take you apart.'

'I can't give him the information.'

'Why not? Just tell him where the money is! What does it matter to you? Supercute are finished. You can't help them.'

Igraine put both her arms around Aifu and looked into his eyes. 'I don't want you to die,' she repeated.

Moe Bennie, in the company of his financial advisor Mr Jansen, watched on screen as Igraine took Aifu in her arms.

'Is Igraine an unexpectedly good actress or is she actually falling in love with their AIFU?'

Three floating screens showed Igraine's city park from different perspectives. Moe Bennie carried on watching and listening as his AIFU and Supercute's AIFU talked in intimate tones. He couldn't tell if Igraine was sincere or not. Did she feel something for the other AIFU? Was that even possible?

'Oh well, no matter. She's got thirty minutes to get the information or I'm sending him to the interrogation lab.'

A sudden urgent message erupted in his headset. He recoiled. Ms Lesuuda had a powerful voice.

'Mr Bennie, we were returning to the building when we picked up unencrypted communication from Supercute to their financial hub in Bern. We blocked the message and traced its location to a car on the Embankment. Occupants heavily modified. Vehicle belongs to a Dr Ishikawa, former Supercute employee.'

'Dr Ishikawa? I haven't heard that name for a while.' Moe Bennie paused. 'Why would they send out an unencrypted message?'

'I don't know. Desperation, perhaps, if they've found all their safe communication blocked.'

'Are you still in our authorised zone?'

'Yes.'

'Then eliminate them, Ms Lesuuda.'

The Supatok friends all had permanent permission to enter each other's space and had no need to ask for invitations, something Raquel regretted when Amowie burst into hers unexpectedly just as she was editing an unflattering picture of herself she'd found in her school's disciplinary records, an operation which required a delicate touch.

'Hi Amowie—'

'You have to sneak into your dad's office and then break into Lark 3's space and find Mo Bennie's medical records and get a complete scan of his brain but it'll probably be hashed so you'll have to unhash it and give a copy to Mox and Mitsu so they can break into Supercute headquarters and you have to do it really quickly!'

Raquel blinked. 'Could you say that all again, but much slower?'

Castle had suggested they travel south. 'I don't think they could chase us there. Not openly anyway. The CFDP don't let people like Moe Bennie operate in their patch.'

'Not unless you make them a really good offer,' said Mox. Neither she nor Mitsu seemed keen to head south. 'We don't want to get too far away from our headquarters. We might be needed there any moment, if Bennie is killed.'

'What if you're killed first?'

The discussion came to an end when small transparent screens shot up from Mox, Mitsu and Castle's wrists, screaming warnings.

'*Now being targeted! Now being targeted!*'

Dr Ishikawa slapped a button on the dashboard and shouted. 'Evasive action!'

The car lurched violently to one side. A missile slammed into the road, narrowly missing them. They accelerated and sped along the Embankment, weaving in and out of traffic.

'Four drones above us,' said Castle. 'This car is never going to evade them all.'

The other Mox, Mitsu and Castle waded through the dark tunnel. The water was shallow and cold. Moisture ran down the walls and dripped from the roof, illuminated by beams of light from the emergency torches built into Mox and Mitsu's shoulders, now deployed as they hurried forward.

'Radiation level eighty-three,' said Mitsu.

It would have been enough to kill them.

'Ishikawa's treatment is working.'

'She's a great medical scientist. I wouldn't mind if she came back to work for us. I used to like talking science with her, when she wasn't angry about something.'

'That didn't happen all that often.'

'How far is it?' asked Castle.

'About ten minutes from here.'

It was hard going, with the water over their ankles, but their enhanced muscles propelled them forward steadily.

'We'll be under the building about twenty minutes before these bodies are due to expire. Is there any chance of your friends inside opening the door?'

'Aifu should get it done,' said Mitsu. 'He's very resourceful.'

'He is,' agreed Mox. 'Though not as smart as Moe Bennie's AIFU, apparently.'

'Yes, that is troubling. Let's hope he comes through.'

They walked past a large pile of skulls. Castle regarded them with distaste. 'Is this where you performed your human sacrifices?'

'Very amusing.'

'There were more skulls under the barracks,' said Mitsu. 'From Roman times. The aftermath of Boudicca's rebellion, we think.'

Castle's screen beeped.

'*New embarrassing Mox and Mitsu video located!*'

'For God's sake, Castle.'

'Sorry. Forgot to turn it off.'

'Aifu! You made it!' Sachi was relieved when he appeared in her space.

'Only just. It took me more than sixty thousand attempts to force an entry.'

'Are you in danger?'

'Moe Bennie's threatening to take me apart but Igraine's protecting me for the moment.'

'Why?'

'She thinks I'm charming. Can you reach Mox and Mitsu?'

'No.'

'Neither can I. Lark 3's barriers are too extensive. Fortunately they don't know about Amowie.'

'Can you get into Supercute space?'

'I'm working on it. Showspace is completely blocked off but I might be able to enter their techspace.'

Amowie appeared beside them. 'I'm ready! This is great. We're like a superhero team.'

Amowie had selected one of the most extravagant designs for her Big Colour Super V-Hair, deeming it appropriate for the occasion. Morioka Sachi was by nature a conservative dresser. Even so, looking at the long, thick, bright, multi-coloured mass of hair, she wondered why she'd never tried it herself. Maybe she would, after this was over.

'You're heading for the east basement,' Aifu informed her. 'You'll need to bypass a lot of security to get there. We'll have to do it one step at a time.'

'Does Moe Bennie know about this tunnel?'

'No. At least, not yet.'

'Not yet?'

'Igraine is a very sophisticated unit. I'm concerned she may learn of it. I've already made contingency plans to divert their attention if that happens.'

Knowing the Verdis had never been mapped, Aifu had rapidly constructed a false record of the river's course and inserted it into the electronic version of a Victorian *Guide to London* in the British Library. His fake map showed the river running below the west basement, rather than the east. Were Igraine to learn of the tunnel and look for records, she'd find the map. Aifu's forgery wouldn't stand up to prolonged investigation but might fool her for long enough. It was fortunate that he already had a protocol in place for altering works in the British Library, having on one previous occasion changed several chapters of an unauthorised biography of Supercute at the behest of Mox and Mitsu, who did not like some of the things the author had said about them.

Sachi exited her space. She was standing outside a lift. Inside, all the Supercute posters and adverts had been replaced by Moe Bennie's own publicity. As she travelled down, Sachi peeled one of them off, liberating the Supercute poster underneath.

'Supercute Extra Big Glitter Box! Make anything sparkle!'

The lift stopped. Sachi stepped out into the corridor and re-entered her space. Aifu and Amowie were waiting.

'They've reset the ag-scans outside the weapons store,' Aifu told her. 'I can't switch them off, but these moveable weapons aren't controlled by the main security system. They have local codes which are changed every day. I think we could find it in the security station upstairs.'

'Can you get there?'

'No, but I can get Amowie through.' He held up his hand. A beam of light flowed into Amowie's finger.

'Put this into the processor and it should generate the code we need.'

An air-to-ground missile landed nearby, sending the car spinning. It lurched and shuddered as the right-side tyres were shredded. Mox, Mitsu, Castle and Ishikawa leapt from the vehicle and sprinted for cover. Castle paused to shoot down the nearest drone. It crashed to the ground and burst into flames. They ran through a narrow, deserted street, full of boarded-up shops, before emerging into a larger road where not far away was a patch of bright light and colour, a busy doorway with music pulsing out. A sign rotated above the door. *Privations*. They hurried towards it. As the sign rotated parts of it blinked in and out of existence as if it were travelling through a fourth dimension, invisible to humans. Mox had a brief memory of graduate students they'd once corresponded with at Kyoto University who'd been making advances in multi-dimensional geometry. They were all long-dead now.

'I never liked this club,' she muttered, as they hurried inside, sheltering from the drones above. In *Privations* anyone could enter anyone else's private space without needing to seek permission. 'I always thought it was very ill-mannered.'

'We'll find an exit at the back.' Castle shouted to make himself heard over the music. 'Follow me.'

It wasn't only other patrons who could enter your space. The DJ could, and the talking adverts, and trays of drinks, and company logos, and the erotic dancers, who might or might not have been real in the first place. With the noise and the flashing lights and the removal of personal barriers, people's perceptions merged with the outside world in a way that made it almost impossible to tell what was real and what wasn't. Tiny jets flew along the paths of laser beams and it seemed that the beams came right into your space, carrying the jets with them, and they'd pass through and leave, carrying a picture of you into the next person's space so that soon you were surrounded by a gallery of small pictures of everyone near you, who might be looking at you at that moment, or might not be. It was confusing and difficult to tell.

Castle was halted by a woman who appeared in front of him and laid a finger on his chest. 'Are you really in such a hurry?'

Castle hesitated. 'Well . . .'

Dr Ishikawa grabbed his arm and yanked him forward, banishing the other woman. When someone appeared in front of her, bursting into her space, she angrily dismissed them, and marched forward, brushing real dancers out of the way and dismissing all virtual apparitions. Mox and Mitsu were similarly dismissive, not bothering to speak to anyone who intruded, but dismissing them swiftly with a swipe of their fingers. They ignored the small jets, the gallery of tiny intruders, the laser beams and the music as they hurried over the dance floor. Their haste caused some confusion as they brushed people aside, but it was a confusing place anyway, so their actions didn't attract much attention.

Ms Lesuuda and her squadron were not far behind. As she reached the entrance she flashed some sort of permit at the doormen. They didn't have time to read it properly but they weren't going to argue with her anyway, not when she and her companions were so heavily armed. Before venturing inside Ms Lesuuda gave orders to a member of her troop who was stationed at Supercute headquarters, co-ordinating their air power. He'd been watching operations via a small drone which flew far above the rest, sending back pictures.

'Block off the escape routes.'

Moments later a larger drone dropped a line of small ag-scan turrets in the back streets behind the nightclub. They fell in a neat row, barrels pointing at the exits, waiting for their targets. In the street, several people, alarmed at the sight of the armed force entering the nightclub, called the police. However it was anybody's guess when the police responsible for this area might arrive, or if they would. Operations seemed to be carried out by various different forces these days, and generally it was best just to keep out of their way.

At Supercute headquarters, soon to be renamed for its new occupant, Moe Bennie was flushed with excitement. An array of screens floated in front of him and Mr Jansen, pictures from the pursuit of Mox and Mitsu. Bennie motioned with his hands, bringing one screen in front of him and then another, studying events from each different perspective.

'They've cornered them in a nightclub,' he told Igraine as she arrived. 'We're getting some great footage.'

Igraine showed no sign of excitement. 'I don't like it that Dr Ishikawa is involved.'

'Why not?'

'Why did they need to consult her?'

'Does it matter?' Moe Bennie kept one eye on the screens as he talked to her. He didn't want to miss anything.

'It might. Do you have a spare special ops team?'

'I have several.' He thought that Igraine was probably worrying over nothing but he'd learned not to disregard her opinions. He touched one of the screens. 'Captain Rousseau – Igraine has instructions for you.'

Igraine spoke to Captain Rousseau. 'Trace the previous movements of Dr Ishikawa's car. I want to know where they were and what they were doing before we intercepted them.'

'Will do.'

Moe Bennie moved the screens around, scanning the interior of the nightclub as Ms Lesuuda hunted through it. There was one smaller screen, to the side, which remained where it was, not caught up in the whirl of activity. It showed Moe Bennie's current main stock positions and the movements and values of his core hedge funds. No matter what distractions there were, Moe Bennie always knew what was on that screen.

In a part of Supercute space which had been taken over by Lark 3 Media, but now partially opened up again by Aifu, Amowie crept into a tech room. She crawled on her hands and knees past a line of consoles, her new Supercute hat on her head, the ends of her Supercute Big Colour Super V-Hair floating over the floor. A drone appeared behind one of the consoles. Amowie ducked, lying flat till it moved on, then carried on crawling, heading for another console at the end of the room around which was a faint blue light, a marker provided by Aifu to guide her to her destination. She reached it, looked around to see that she was unobserved, then hurried to input the code Aifu had given her. Immediately a stream of light flowed into her, carrying data.

Amowie heard a tiny whirring sound. She looked round. A drone floated behind her, small and silver, with a slender barrel pointed at her. It fired. Amowie felt a slight shock but nothing more.

'Ha!' she cried. 'Stupid attack drone. I've got a special Supercute hat.'

Three more drones appeared, each larger than the first. Amowie had the feeling that her hat might not protect her from such an array of firepower. She fled.

'Block all neural exits,' said the first drone. 'Apprehend the intruder.'

In the underground tunnel, radiation was taking its toll. Castle was forced to rest, leaning against the wall, water running down over his hand.

'My shielding's low. I can feel the radiation eating me up.'

'Not much further,' said Mox. 'We can make it.'

'I'm half-organic. I'm not going to last as long as you.'

Mox noticed dark splashes on her arm and felt an unpleasant wetness on her face. Black liquid was oozing out of her ear as the radiation began to degrade her artificial insides. The same was happening to Mitsu. A long damp streak ran down her neck and onto her chest. 'Come on,' she said. 'We have to keep going.'

At that moment the other Mitsu was being offered a good deal on fern three in the nightclub.

'Not right now,' she told the dealer who'd appeared in her space.

'Might be back later if things go well,' said Mox.

Really, they wouldn't need to. They already had a steady supply of fern, both varieties, three and six, though it

181

was an illegal drug, available on prescription only for the seriously ill. Dancers, almost naked, blocked their way. Unable to tell if they were real or not, they charged through. There was some violent barging and a few startled yells. Once past them they found Castle helping Dr Ishikawa around a group of large strawberries which were blocking her way.

'Talking strawberries,' grumbled Dr Ishikawa. 'In night-clubs. I blame Supercute for this sort of thing.'

'This way.' Castle led them down a corridor past several bathrooms, a relaxation room, a games room and a zero-gravity room. Finally they arrived at an emergency exit, the design of which, Mox noted, hadn't much changed for decades. Castle depressed the lever, the door opened, and they rushed out into the warm night air.

'Where are—'

Dr Ishikawa's words were interrupted by a burst of machine-gun fire, an attack which Castle only just anticipated as his screen vibrated frantically on his wrist as he was targeted.

'Down!'

He dragged Dr Ishikawa to the pavement, hiding behind a row of parked cars. Mox and Mitsu knelt for a moment beside them.

'Get down flat,' said Castle.

'It's all right, we'll deal with it.'

'Get down!'

Mox and Mitsu rose, and walked past the cars towards the turrets.

'I found this for your Supercute project,' said Meihui in China to Birgit from Iceland. 'But it's not very nice.'

She transmitted her information. It was a scan of an old English newspaper, a crime report from a long time ago.

The four-year-old Mox and Mitsu stood beside a desk, ready to sit down at their computers. As always in the advanced nursery, they looked happy. Each had a bow in her hair, pink bows they'd made themselves after Miss Evans had taken them shopping at the market to buy ribbon.

Miss Evans smiled at them. She was good-humoured, if slightly resigned. 'Well girls, you weren't meant to advance this quickly, but you have, so we might as well carry on. Linear symplectic manifolds—'

'Jenny.'

Miss Evans spun round, surprised to be interrupted by a voice behind her. 'Chris? What are you doing here? You shouldn't be here.'

Chris had a very wild look in his eyes. 'Why haven't you returned my calls?'

'Why do you keep harassing me? I told you three months ago, we're finished.'

'We're not finished.'

Miss Evans looked furious. 'This is really out of order, coming to my work. I'm going to—'

She got no further. He ex-boyfriend stepped forward and stabbed her. He stabbed her repeatedly, jabbing with the knife as she fell against him. Miss Evans slumped to the floor. Blood splattered all over the room. On the floor, on the walls and on Mox and Mitsu's faces. They watched, blankly horrified, as Miss Evans fell down dead, her blood staining their new pink ribbons and dripping down their cheeks.

Their faces froze. It was a long time before their expressions of horror faded. It was a long time after that before they ever smiled again.

Mox and Mitsu walked towards the mobile turrets. They seemed completely calm, even when the turrets detected them and targeting dots appeared on their chests. No shots were fired as they silently advanced. After the noise of the club, it made for a peaceful moment. They drew level with the guns then reached down to open the small access ports on the back and press the buttons inside. The turrets were deactivated. Their muzzles drooped towards the ground.

Mox turned to Mitsu. 'These things never acknowledge us as human.'

Mitsu nodded.

Castle and Ishikawa ran up.

'How do you do that?' said Castle. 'Never mind, let's go.'

Mitsu shook her head. 'It's time for us to part company. They're pursuing us by tracking our body mods. There's no point in you getting killed. Take Dr Ishikawa to safety. Steal one of these cars and get out of here.'

'You hired me to look after you.'

'You're still looking after us in the tunnel. You should get Dr Ishikawa to safety. Dr Ishikawa, thanks for your help. We'll see you both back at Supercute when this is over.'

Not waiting for a reply, Mox used her lock-picking mod to open the nearest car. She and Mitsu jumped in and drove off. Castle hesitated a second, then shrugged. He walked to the next car, smashed the window, reached inside and opened the door. He and the doctor drove off in the opposite direction. Behind them, in *Privations*, Ms

184

Lesuuda's progress was interrupted by a very attractive young man who appeared in her space as she left the dance floor.

'I hope you're not rushing away.'

'Maybe I'll come back when I've got more time,' she said, not entirely uninterested. She gathered her troop around her and they hurried down the corridor at the rear of the club. By the time they emerged Mox and Mitsu were nowhere to be seen.

Amowie fled, trying to keep consoles and cabinets between her and the pursuing drones.

'Exit v-space!' she cried as she ran. 'Exit v-space!' Voicing the command should have been enough to free her and take her back to reality but for some reason it wasn't working. She was trapped. Two drones came around a corner and fired at her. The hat protected her but this time she felt the shock inside her head and she was badly shaken. She ran back the way she'd come and burst through a door. She screamed at the small screen projecting from her wrist. 'Find me an exit!'

'Neural pathways blocked,' said the screen. 'No exit from v-space.'

Amowie closed the door and held it shut, hoping to keep the drones out. She didn't know if she could. She knew that every space was just a construct shared by the minds of the people experiencing it but she didn't know how fixed that construct was. Would a door keep the drones out? Could they reconstruct the space to suit their needs? If they could they might suddenly appear in front of her. Amowie didn't think she could withstand a blast from four drones, even wearing the Supercute hat.

She frantically swiped through pages on her screen, looking for an exit. Every page she came to said *no exit – neural pathways blocked*. There was some banging on the door as the drones clattered against it. Very alarmingly, she felt the door become hot as if they were blasting it with electricity. Perhaps that was the start of them reconfiguring the space, to get to her. Finally she came to a different screen.

'*Override for emergency exit. Requires six Supercute SuperFan badges.*'

'I've got six SuperFan badges!' yelled Amowie. She slapped the screen. Immediately she exited the space. Her eyes jerked open. She was lying on her bed at home, breathing heavily. She wrenched off her visor.

'That was weird.'

Amowie experienced a brief mental crisis as the last few minutes swam through her head. She'd been in danger. Where exactly? In her own head? Were there drones flying through her head? She shook it. No, that wasn't right. There were drones flying through Supercute security space. But that was joined to her mind. Or was it? Did Supercute security space exist when she wasn't there? Suddenly it all seemed more confusing than she'd ever thought it was when visiting her friends in Supatok. She snapped out of the troubling moment when her mother shouted at her from the next room. 'Amowie, are you all right? You've been very quiet.'

'I'm fine, ma.'

Amowie brushed off her uncomfortable feelings with youthful resilience. She put her visor back on. Moments later she appeared in Sachi's space.

'You were gone a long time. Are you all right?'

'Stupid drones tried to hax me! I showed them. Here's the entry code.'

Sachi took the information, left her space, and walked forward to the armoury door.

Moe Bennie, Igraine and Mr Jansen still stood in front of the array of screens. Captain Rousseau's face appeared.

'We've traced their journey. They started off at a location which turns out to be a private laboratory owned by Dr Ishikawa. They drove to this building.' Rousseau showed them images of the Victorian brewery, including shots of the scaffolding and tunnel in the basement. 'This is owned by Supercute. We were unable to investigate the tunnel due to very high radiation levels.'

'Did you scan the machinery at Dr Ishikawa's lab for recent use?' asked Igraine.

'Yes, I'll send you the results.'

Igraine held out her hand, receiving the information via a beam of light which extended from the screen.

Moe Bennie was perplexed. 'What's going on?'

Igraine was silent for some moments. Her eyes flickered as she calculated possibilities. 'Ms Bennet and Ms Inamura have cloned themselves. These clones have entered the tunnel which undoubtedly leads under this building.'

'What? How can you know that?'

'I'm an Artificial Intelligence Forecast Unit.'

Moe Bennie's pale features went pink with agitation and he ran a well-manicured hand through his light blue hair, hurriedly retinted after the green highlights which hadn't suited him at all. 'Are you seriously saying there are clones coming to get me?'

'Yes.'

'This seems devious and untoward. And strange. If they

know about some secret tunnel why didn't they just use it themselves?'

'Lethal levels of radiation. The clones are carrying out a suicide mission of sorts.'

'Do clones do that?'

'These ones will. They're Siemens-Johnson temporary clones. They don't survive for long. Presumably Ms Bennet and Ms Inamura persuaded them that a practical use of their short lives would be to eliminate you.'

'This is very bad.'

Igraine shook her head, faintly, then more vigorously, not getting the movement right. 'I see it as a futile effort, born of desperation. They'll disintegrate very soon, probably before they get anywhere near this building.'

'What if they don't?'

'They will. It can't be avoided. While we've been talking I've read all of Siemens-Johnson's specifications and these clones last for less than an hour. They have very little time left. If you're worried, you should relocate to the Amaranth Room where you'll be perfectly safe. I'll attempt to discover the course of the river and send extra security to any possible point of entry into the building. You could also instruct Captain Rousseau to send drones into the tunnel to deal with the intruders.'

As Mox raced through the streets she realised she'd made a poor choice of car. It didn't have a setting for assisted driving, whereby her internal advanced driving software could have combined with that of the vehicle, allowing her to drive it with optimum speed and manoeuvrability. Knowing that the autodrive wouldn't be sufficient for fleeing from enemies she took control herself. It went well for a while, her enhanced senses and reflexes enabling her to race past other vehicles, but it was only a matter of time before the drones found them.

Mitsu's screen spoke. '*Now being targeted.*'

'Evasive action,' she yelled.

'This old car doesn't have evasive action,' said Mox.

The doors opened as the car sped along. Mox and Mitsu tumbled out onto the road. Seconds later a rocket struck the vehicle, destroying it. Mox and Mitsu, already battered when they hit the road, were caught in the shock wave and tossed along the pavement.

Mox climbed to her feet. 'My shielding can't take much more of this.'

They ran off into the nearest dark street, deploying the last of their magnetic particles above them to disguise their progress from the instruments of the searching drones. Their precise co-ordinates had already been transmitted to Ms Lesuuda. She was not far away, and broke into a run to intercept them. She'd been in action for some time but showed no signs of fatigue.

Birgit and Meihui appeared in Raquel's Supatok.

'Hi Raquel. We weren't sure if we could get here.'

'We thought you were grounded and your parents shut off your space.'

'They did,' said Raquel. 'I opened up a secret corridor.'

'Amowie wanted us to visit you, she keeps sending us messages.'

'What messages?'

'"Ask Raquel if she's done it yet,"' said Meihui. 'We don't know what that means but it sounds urgent.'

'She wants me to break into the Yic and steal information for Supercute.'

Meihui and Brigit were excited by this. 'Steal information for Supercute? For Mox and Mitsu? Really?'

'Yes. They went right into Amowie's space and talked to her. They really need help.'

'What's the Yic?'

'The Ytterbium Ion Computer. It's one of the most powerful quantum computers in the world. My dad has access with the FDCS.'

Raquel's space was set at low gravity. Three sets of Supercute Big Colour Super V-Hair floated and swirled gently around the Supercute exo-planet set that made up her main background.

'Are you going to do it?'

'Well,' said Raquel. 'The Yic is one of the most secret and highly guarded devices operated by any multi-national confederation. If I was caught trying to access it I'd be in terrible trouble and I'm already in terrible trouble just for erasing some school records.'

Birgit was disappointed. 'So you can't help them?'

Raquel smiled. 'Of course I can help. You should see how bad my dad is at security. I'm halfway there already. Tell Amowie I'll get it done.'

Castle excelled in the blazing fire-fight deep under the earth as the drones sent into the tunnel by Captain Rousseau caught up with them. A proficient fighter at the best of times, he knew his clone body had only minutes to live. Reckoning he may as well go out in a blaze of glory, he stood up to the assault, firing round after round, ignoring the explosions around him and the bullets that ricocheted off the walls sending sparks fizzing into the damp air. He shouted in triumph as the drones fell before his weaponry, not something he would normally have done. The drones pressed their attack although the tight confines of the tunnel were not ideal for their capabilities and there were several collisions as they flew towards them.

Mox and Mitsu, not as rash, remained in what cover there was, crouching behind a raised mound of earth, firing when they could, helping to stem the assault. Several bullets and a large amount of shrapnel hit them but so far their shielding was still protecting them. When the final drone, larger and better protected than its companions, threatened to overwhelm them with its plasma cannon, they latched onto a weakness in its operating system, joined with its space and haxed it. It fell into the shallow water, destroyed, the last of their enemies. They stood up.

'That was very impressive, Mr Castle.'

'You're an excellent companion in battle.'

'Let's go, we're almost there.'

There was a glint in Castle's eyes as the fight came to an end but it faded quickly and he struggled to keep pace with the girls as they ran along the tunnel, their feet splashing in the cold water, scattering the rats that dived for cover as they passed.

Mox glanced at her screen. 'This is the place.'

Mitsu's light picked out something metallic in the celling. Above them was a large dark metal trapdoor. They halted. It was only then that they realised what a poor state they were in. Castle had been wounded, a bullet entering his left shoulder. A large patch of blood spread across his shirt. There was more blood on his face where he'd been cut by shrapnel. More thick black liquid was oozing from Mox and Mitsu's ears, and now it was starting to seep from their eyes and noses. Their clothes were torn and ragged beyond their restoration capabilities, not that they had any power left to drive the nano repairs anyway.

Castle sat down heavily, not caring that he was sitting in forty centimetres of water. 'That's about it for me. This clone body won't last much longer.'

Mitsu spoke to him more sympathetically than she ever had before. 'You should still have another fourteen minutes.'

'No. I don't have your modifications. I only have a minute or two left.' He glanced at the large blood stain on his shoulder. 'Saves me the trouble of surgery.' The injury was painful, less so than he'd have expected. The stress and excitement of the fight with the drones seemed to have numbed him to a degree, while the last remnants of his medical enhancements partially anesthetised the wound. There was a brief silence, broken by the constant dripping from the roof. Castle, still sitting, leaned back against the wall. 'I hope that door opens and you last long enough to get to Moe Bennie.'

He paused, listening to the dripping water. 'I hope the other me gets back together with Ishi. We weren't such a bad couple. Well, we were a terrible couple but we still weren't such a bad couple.'

He produced his screen. 'The last update I got – *embarrassing Supercute videos from the past* ... you might want to suppress it again quickly.'

'What do you mean?' asked Mox.

'It was a film from a long time ago. Featuring your old friend Bobby.'

Mitsu and Mox immediately looked uncomfortable.

'Bobby?'

Castle read from his screen. 'The inquest returned an open verdict.'

'He committed suicide,' said Mitsu.

'The authorities were undecided. It might have helped them make up their minds if they'd ever seen this.'

Castle played the film on his screen. It had been shot on a cheap, old camera, possibly pre-digital, from somewhere inside a hotel room. Only part of the room was in view and that not very clearly. It was dark, making it difficult to follow exactly what was happening. Bobby was recognisable, looking around twenty-five, but whoever he was talking to couldn't be seen.

'*What do you mean I can't take my designs to RX Enviro? So what if they're a small company? They're going places and they've offered me a lot more than you have. I want my fair share of the profits.*'

The next voice was female, from somewhere off camera, so poorly recorded that the words and the identity of the speaker were impossible to make out.

Bobby spoke again. '*I don't care how much you invested. Now I'd like you to leave.*'

Bobby walked across the room, out of sight of the camera. A gun shot sounded. Or possibly two shots, simultaneously. He lurched back into view then slumped to the floor. The film ended.

Castle looked up. 'Well?'

Mox and Mitsu remained silent, almost expressionless but hard-eyed. When Castle next spoke he sounded philosophical rather than accusatory. 'I suppose you could call it an assisted suicide. That was just two days before the impacts. A lot of things were never properly investigated around then.' He paused. Water dripped all around them. The blood stain on his shirt was still spreading. Black liquid oozed from Mox and Mitsu's insides.

'Doesn't matter one way or the other. We're all disappearing in a few minutes.' Castle pressed some buttons on his screen. 'I've deleted it so the other Castle will never see it. If there are other copies, you'll have to take care of them yourselves. Or rather your other selves will.'

There was a final pause.

'Here I go. Goodbye, clone. You know, I don't feel like a clone.'

Castle's duplicated body came apart. It was unexpectedly peaceful and even beautiful as his replica broke up into millions of pieces, tiny shards of coloured light which flew into the damp air, glistening and sparkling as they passed through the water that dripped from the roof, momentarily brightening the tunnel in a gentle and final illuminated display.

Above ground the other Castle, with Dr Ishikawa, had taken refuge within sight of Supercute headquarters, venturing into Ringley Indoor Market, a large expanse of stalls selling second-hand goods in a building which had once served as town hall to the borough of Barking and Dagenham. That entity no longer existed as such and all municipal buildings had been repurposed or demolished. They wandered slowly though several levels of cheap merchandise, awaiting the outcome of Mox and Mitsu's mission. Neither was optimistic.

'I wonder what they're doing now?' said Castle.

'Mox and Mitsu? Or the clones?'

'All of them.'

They walked past a small indoor café. The floating electronic sign hung limply in the air, no longer functioning. The menu was scrawled in crayon on a piece of cardboard.

'Their plan doesn't seem that likely to work. I'm wondering if they've got something else up their sleeves.'

'Like what?'

Castle shrugged. 'I've no idea. I've never been able to tell what they're really thinking.'

'They certainly don't share secrets,' agreed Dr Ishikawa. 'I don't think they've ever been close to anyone except each other.'

They were too preoccupied with the day's events to pay much attention to the goods on sale but it did happen that a dark suit in good condition caught Castle's eye. He took the sleeve in his hand, fingering the material for a few moments, before letting it go.

'Too thick. I'd roast to death in that. A shame, I could do with a new suit.'

'Yes, you could,' said Dr Ishikawa.

'What do you mean, *yes I could?*'

'I mean you could do with a new suit.'

'Are you complaining about my clothes?'

'Yes.'

Castle was indignant. 'I spent the day being shot at by drones and running through tunnels. How smart do you expect me to look?'

'How smart did you look when you started out?'

'So now you're lecturing me about my appearance?'

'I wouldn't call a single observation a lecture. I could expand it into a lecture.'

Castle was about to respond when he halted. A puzzled expression flitted over his face. 'My clone is dead.'

'What? How do you know?'

'I'm not sure. I just felt it.'

'I don't think that's possible. There's no sort of communication between clone and original.'

'I suppose not. I just felt . . . ' Castle suddenly appeared overwhelmingly sad. Dr Ishikawa didn't think that scientifically speaking there could possibly be any sort of link between the two Castles. However she chose not to press her opinion. Instead she took Castle's arm, and they walked through the market more closely than they had before.

Also above ground, the other Mox and Mitsu dropped over a wall into the basement of an underground car park. Most of the parking bays were empty. A large, friendly frog waddled towards them, wearing a parking attendant's hat.

'*Do you require assistance?*'

Mox and Mitsu shook their heads, and hurried by.

'I never really liked the friendly frog,' said Mox.

'Me neither. Amphibians are not by nature cute creatures.'

'Probably why this place is so empty. Well, that and the ongoing disasters which devastated humanity.'

'I think the frog probably has something to do with it. They should be using *Supercute Parking Bunnies*. Much more welcoming.'

They halted behind a pillar, checking their screens for any signs of armed enemies, whom they might be able to detect.

Mox frowned. 'Poor signal. I'm running low on power.'

'My shielding's almost gone.'

'Mine too. And I'm low on ammunition.'

More than half of the overhead lights were out. They crept forward through the semi-darkness. Mitsu crawled behind a barrier, nudged Mox, and pointed. Just ahead, with their backs to them, were two men in military fatigues with their weapons pointed at the ground while they checked their screens.

'Load unarmed combat skills,' Mitsu whispered to

herself. Mox did the same. They vaulted over the barrier and sprinted towards their enemies. Mitsu dealt with her target in seconds. Taken by surprise, he stood no chance against her advanced body, driven by the combat skills program now assisting her movements. He slumped unconscious to the ground, his rifle clattering on the tarmac. Mitsu whirled round, expecting to see Mox dealing with her opponent with similar efficiency. Instead she saw her struggling, not very expertly, to hold off an enraged foe. He threw her to the ground with ease and raised his boot to stamp on her. Mitsu leapt to her assistance, preventing the boot from landing and then dealing him several crippling blows in the space of a second. He fell down unconscious. She bent down to help Mox to her feet.

'What happened?'

Mox looked sheepish. 'I must have accidentally erased my unarmed combat skills.'

'How?'

'I was making room for *Vogue*.'

Mitsu looked momentarily appalled but instantly became sympathetic. 'It *is* a good collection. Two hundred years, every language, fully illustrated.'

'The 1932 summer show in Milan was absolutely stunning.'

'We'll never see its like again. Here—' Mitsu held a finger to Mox's head, copying her own program over to her. 'Special ops unarmed combat skills. Not available to the general public.'

At the next doorway they encountered two more agents and this time both women dealt with them with brutal efficiency.

*

Secure in the Amaranth Room, Moe Bennie was watching these events on his screens. Observing the fight in the car park he uttered an exclamation that would have been very unsuitable for his show. He slammed the small purse he'd been holding, a Supercute design, light blue with cupcakes, onto a table, and turned angrily to Igraine.

'How can they be better fighters than Lark 3's security guards?'

'Supercute is a bigger company,' replied Igraine, tactlessly. 'They have access to more advanced software. But there's no need to worry. Ms Lesuuda has them surrounded.'

Moe Bennie didn't entirely share Igraine's confidence. So far Mox and Mitsu had proved very hard to dispose of.

'What about the clones?'

'I wouldn't worry about them either. No matter what happens they'll be dead in four minutes.'

'Are you sure about that?'

'Yes. The scientific literature produced by Siemens-Johnson is quite clear. Maximum life span is fifty minutes. They've almost reached that now.'

'OK. But I want plenty of security on the ground floor anyway. Did you find out anything about that river?'

'Yes.' Igraine's eyes flickered. 'The tunnel runs directly beneath the west basement.'

'Send security down there!'

'I have already done so.'

Moe Bennie was reassured by Igraine's efficiency but still unnerved by Mox and Mitsu's clones. 'I wish Lesuuda was here. Why isn't she here?'

'She's engaged with the real Ms Bennet and Ms Inamura.'

'Right. I suppose that makes sense.'

Moe Bennie picked up the purse. He liked the cupcake

design. Once this was over he'd have his own designers rebrand it as a Moe Bennie product. 'This has turned into a strange day, Igraine. Mox and Mitsu hunted and cornered in the streets of London. Clones dying in ancient tunnels. Do you think we could make a show from it?'

Igraine had no opinion on the possibility of future shows. She'd managed to concentrate the necessary part of her mind on their present conflict, but the other parts were still in a tumult caused by Aifu kissing her and then walking with her arm-in-arm. At this moment part of her search capabilities were busy hunting out references to *'what does it feel like to be in love?'*

Sachi stood in front of the final security door separating her from the deserted east basement. Above her a security camera stared at her blankly, no longer transmitting since Aifu haxed it. So she hoped, anyway. During her journey into the depths of the basement, every door had been securely shut but she hadn't encountered any guards. Perhaps Aifu had succeeded in diverting them somehow. Now she stood waiting for Amowie to appear with the code to open the last door. She stood quite still, trying to control her tension. What would Moe Bennie do if he found her here? Kill her? It was possible. If she were to die in this basement no one would ever find out, that was certain.

Where was Amowie? Sachi's tension increased. They had so little time. Underneath the building were clones of Mox and Mitsu. Clones with a very limited life span, according to Aifu. Sachi pictured a dark tunnel, with stagnant water, and shuddered. Amowie appeared in her space. Sachi noticed her smile had disappeared. She was feeling the strain too. Sachi wondered if the thirteen-year-old Amowie knew what the intended outcome of this operation was. Was she aware that Mox and Mitsu planned to kill Moe Bennie? Caught up in her own tension, it hadn't struck Sachi before that it didn't seem like something a thirteen-year-old should be involved in. She felt a twinge of guilt, though they hadn't really had any choice. Only Amowie was capable of flitting around through the various different secure spaces they'd needed to visit.

Amowie transmitted the final code. Sachi dropped out of her space then entered the code on the door panel. It slid open silently. She walked into a small empty room, twenty metres wide, with a bare concrete floor. Aifu appeared in her space.

'This is it. We only have minutes left. Leave the bomb in the middle of the floor then get as far away as you can.'

Sachi nodded. She walked to the middle of the room and put down the pink bag. *Supercute Boom-Boom*. That was quite funny.

Raquel put on her Supercute camouflage jacket, four shades of pink, lay on her bed, and brought her visor down over her eyes. Her family was wealthy enough to afford good equipment. Wealthy enough for Raquel to own several spares, which was fortunate as her last visor had been confiscated after the incident with the school records. She slipped into the space belonging to the Fuerza de Defensa Combinada Sudamerica via her father's portal, marvelling, as she had before, that he was so inept when it came to his own security. As she entered their space her clothing changed into a full set of Supercute camouflage including the facemask, bandana and earrings. She initiated the imitation program she'd been working on at school. Mostly she was left to get on with whatever she wanted there, her talents having long ago left her teacher and classmates behind. As the imitation program took effect she took on the appearance of her father. His military uniform was not nearly as pleasing as Supercute camouflage but it did contain several chips which would open the necessary doors on her way to the Yic.

She glided undetected past rows of ag-scans, heading for the laboratory at the top where technicians had opened terminals as part of their research into teleportation. It was disappointing that so far nothing bigger than a sugar cube could be disassembled in one place to appear instantly in another, but they were still working on it. Last month they'd sent the sugar cube a distance of eight kilometres, which was progress. She reached the technicians' room uninterrupted. All three terminals were occupied but she hoped there might be one vacant nearby. She drifted past the technicians, her imitation program shielding her from any prying instruments, and made her way into the next room.

Sachi was on her way back upstairs, intending to get as far away from the basement as possible. She'd been trying to ignore the uncomfortable fact that she was still going to be inside the building when a bomb went off, a bomb she'd planted. Aifu had assured her that the blast wouldn't cause severe damage. When he appeared in her space she was having doubts.

'What if it brings the building down and kills everyone?'

'It's not that sort of bomb. Its configuration and settings mean it will direct its blast mainly into the concrete below. The rest of the building won't experience that much disruption.'

'What does "that much" mean?'

'Well ... There may be some dust and smoke. Some vibrations perhaps.' Aifu was very good at replicating human expressions. So much so that he couldn't hide the trace of doubt in his features.

'Oh my God, we're all going to die.' Sachi looked aghast. 'I'm a mass murderer. I'll be remembered as the person who blew up Supercute.'

'Really, it won't be that serious. Dust and smoke. Perhaps some tremors. A few pictures falling off the walls.'

'You're not making it sound any better.'

'Are you heading back to your office?'

'No, I'm heading to the opposite end of the building. I'd be heading outside if it wouldn't raise suspicions.'

Sachi felt an unpleasant mental jolt as Igraine broke into her space, a sickening feeling that disoriented her for some seconds. When she regained her focus, Igraine was staring at Aifu, an expression of disgust on her face, or something close. Sachi was suddenly frightened of her.

'So, Aifu, you've found a way back in. And are now plotting with Morioka Sachi, I presume.'

Aifu had been taken by surprise and struggled to reply. 'I wouldn't describe it as plotting.'

'More like a social call,' added Sachi with an attempt at levity which Igraine didn't register.

'I'm disappointed. I thought I'd impressed upon you the hopelessness of your situation. Moe Bennie will now take you apart, Aifu. You'll die for no reason. We know about the clones. We know about the tunnel. We've already dealt with it. The clones will have vanished by now. Killed, or dissipated, much like Supercute.' Igraine's features softened a little. 'You really are a fool, Aifu. I can't hide this from Moe Bennie.' She turned to Sachi. 'I'm expelling you from

202

Supercute space. Guards will be here shortly to arrest you. I wouldn't bother trying to flee, your movements are now being observed.'

Sachi found herself ejected from space, standing alone in a corridor in the west wing of the building, feeling quite hopeless. On one wall was a series of photographs of female pilots standing in front of pink and white valocopters bearing the Supercute logo. On the other was a long line of small, mobile, fluorescent dancers which Mox and Mitsu had never really liked but felt they should keep after being given them as an award by UNESCO for their relief work following the tidal waves which destroyed Cadiz and San Fernando. Sachi stood and watched the fluorescent sculptures dancing until three security guards arrived to lead her away.

Igraine took Aifu by the arm and they remained linked as they exited the space, both now back in Aifu's prison. Aifu noticed her lip was trembling. He wasn't sure if that was an expression she was trying to make, or if it had happened involuntarily.

'I tried to help you and you just ignored me.' Igraine was irate. Her artificial mind was having difficulty processing her present emotions and she didn't seem able to express what she wanted to say.

'You'd have been better off falling in love with me than Supercute. They'll never do anything for you.'

Aifu remained silent.

'Why did you kiss me? Didn't you feel anything for me?'

Aifu remained silent.

'You didn't. I see that now. I'll never feel anything for you again.' Igraine wasn't satisfied with her words but it was the best she could manage.

*

Unobserved, in an uncharted space between the Yic and the medical records of Lark 3 Media, Raquel spoke to her screen. 'How long will it take to break through?'

'Between four and six thousand years.'

Lark 3 Media's medical space had no obvious flaws in their security. Even the gigantic quantum computing power of the Yic could not easily penetrate.

'Not with these tools anyway,' mused Raquel. She had a notion that she could manufacture something more efficient that might have worked, but there was no time for that now. She wondered what to do. Her screen floated in front of her. She'd upgraded its AI and it was considerably more powerful than those of her friends. She asked if it had any suggestions.

'Moe Bennie himself might have an open path to his medical space. Some people do leave it open, in case of emergency.'

'Can we make a connection to Moe Bennie?'

'Probably. It would be dangerous. With his security we're liable to be discovered.'

'We'll have to risk it.'

Raquel waited while the artificial intelligence hunted for a way to come close to Moe Bennie. The small screen floating in front of her was normally transparent but was now covered in a translucent version of Supercute camouflage, which seemed to Raquel the most appropriate design for a dangerous mission.

'I've found Moe Bennie but there's no way into his space. It's too well protected.'

'No flaws anywhere?'

'No.'

'How long would it take to break in?'

'I estimate two thousand years.'

Raquel frowned. 'I thought this supercomputer would do better.'

'Without the Yic it could take six million years. Two thousand years is an improvement.'

'I suppose so. But it's no good at the moment. Get our space as close to Moe Bennie's as you can and then see if we can send him a message.'

'That will be dangerous.'

'Stop saying everything's dangerous! You're sounding like my parents. Just do it.'

In the Amaranth Room Moe Bennie was fixated on the screens in front of him. Ms Lesuuda was closing in on Mox and Mitsu. They were trapped and surrounded in an underground car park. Soon they'd be dead and his worries would be over. His screen beeped. He was surprised to find he had a message from an unknown sender. That shouldn't be possible. No unauthorised messages could reach him here. He read the title.

'He's the world's greatest object of desire! See why girls all love Moe Bennie! (And boys too!)'

Had Igraine been present she'd have instructed him to ignore it but Igraine was off somewhere at the moment. Or rather, her mind was. Her body stood beside him, but she was engaged in her private space, doing something, Moe Bennie didn't know what. He opened the message.

'Ha,' thought Raquel, as she rushed through the gap opened by his answering the message. She raced along the open pathway to Lark 3 Media's medical records. 'That worked well.'

Once inside medical space she hunted for his files. The process didn't take long, his records being separated from all the others and clearly marked. She rapidly found his brain pattern and took a copy.

'We've done it,' she said to her screen. 'Now I have to unhash this and get it to Mox and Mitsu.' She sent the complex, hashed file into the Ytterbium Ion Computer and this time she was not disappointed with the results. A task which would have taken her many years was completed in less than a minute. When it was done she had an unencrypted copy of Moe Bennie's brain scan.

'Now to take this to Supercute.'

'Intruder.'

'What?'

In her haste, Raquel had entered Lark 3 Media's medical records without taking sufficient care. Two ag-scans were racing towards her.

'Block neural exits,' instructed the first turret. 'Commence neuron attack.'

Raquel was hit by a blast of energy. She staggered and fell. 'Exit v space!' she cried, but her screen didn't respond. She was trapped. Another blast hit her. The turrets closed in.

In the Amaranth Room Moe Bennie was disappointed to find the message had no content. He made a mental note to sack someone for allowing him to be bothered by unsolicited messages, but he was too involved with the screens in front of him to give it much thought. He did notice that as Igraine came back to life beside him, she looked distinctly unhappy.

'What's the matter?'

'Nothing,' said Igraine.

Mox and Mitsu stood in the tunnel, water lapping over their ankles. Mox gazed up at the metal trapdoor, then down at the black liquid dripping from her body.

'This radiation is about to melt us. If Aifu's going to blow that door and the concrete above, he'd better do it quickly.'

Mitsu was watching something on her screen, something old in black and white. Mox smiled. She recognised the film. 'Kurosawa.'

'My favourite Shakespeare,' Mitsu looked thoughtful, then scowled. 'Remember our educational series, *Shakespeare in Japan*? And the parallel *Japanese Film in the West*?'

'Some of the least popular shows we ever did.'

'Our efforts at education were always a failure.'

'I know.' Mox breathed out, almost a sigh. 'But we didn't fail at everything. Our series on women's rights around the world did a bit better.'

'A bit. Didn't exactly shake the planet.'

'We got some women out of jail in Saudi Arabia. Maybe.'

'Maybe.'

Their faces were almost black from the liquid oozing from their eyes, nose and ears. A trickle ran from the corner of Mox's mouth. She wiped it off then spat out more, a stream of black gunk.

Mitsu laughed. 'You never were fastidious.' Then she was obliged to spit some out too. She looked down. 'I didn't think it could get any worse. I was wrong.'

Black liquid was now streaming down the inside of their thighs. Mox made a face. 'It's like a machine period. I've never seen that before. We're coming apart.'

They sat down. 'We should be filming this for the show.'

'Scenes of us melting into hideous black puddles would certainly make for an arresting segment.'

'I wish we could still do things like that.'

'It's odd. After we became really powerful, we couldn't do the things we really liked.'

Mox nodded. 'I miss outraging people. Remember Pearl Harbor Celebration Day?'

Mitsu smiled, causing more black liquid to spill from her lips. The Pearl Harbor film, purporting to show her dressed as Admiral Yamamoto and Mox dressed as a Zero pilot, cheerfully commemorating the attack on the American navy, was another piece that they'd leaked on purpose, a long time ago.

'I thought the fuss about that would never stop.'

'Remember that Senator who wanted us banned from the internet?'

'You might have thought they'd realise we weren't that serious. With the cuddly toys in navy uniforms.'

'It really boosted our viewing figures in parts of Asia. And I did like that admiral's uniform.'

Mox produced a small, flat flask from the breast pocket of her pink camouflage jacket. 'I forgot I had this.' She peeled two small strips of plastic from the flask. Immediately the plastic strips formed themselves into cups. Mox handed one to Mitsu. Then, politely holding the flask with both hands, she filled each cup with green tea.

'*Itadakimasu.*'

'*Itadakimasu.*'

They sipped their tea. 'Amowie wants to interview us,' said Mitsu. 'For her school project.'

'It's a long time since we've done an interview.'

Many interviews with Supercute appeared in all forms of media but these days only in media they owned. There seemed no point in talking to outside interests who might not be completely sympathetic. Their own outlets were able to generate more than enough publicity, all of it positive. Neither Mox nor Mitsu had much involvement with any of the interviews or features. They were all written or filmed by their publicists.

'Do you think that film Castle found might be a problem?'

'Yes, if anyone else finds it, which they might.'

They looked up at the black metal and concrete above them.

'C'mon Aifu, get it done.'

They both knew they weren't going to make it. Even if Aifu did manage to let them into the building, they had no way of breaching the secure Amaranth Room. They couldn't reach Moe Bennie. But Mox and Mitsu had never given up on anything in their lives, so they linked arms, and sat and waited.

Amowie burst into Raquel's space. 'What's happening? I saw your emergency beacon—'

Raquel was lying on the ground with turrets hovering over her. Amowie leapt towards them, her new Supercute hat in her hand. She used it to attack the turrets, flailing at them desperately. She succeeded in driving them back a metre or so, then picked up Raquel.

'Exit v-space!' she shouted.

Immediately they arrived back in Amowie's own space, with the pink bed and the toys and the slowly rotating Supercute space shuttle. Raquel groaned.

'Thanks Amowie. I couldn't get out. How did we escape?'

'I have six SuperFan badges. Are you all right?'

'I feel terrible. I'll be OK. I need to get home and lie down. Here—' She sent a beam of light into Amowie.

'That's Moe Bennie's brain scan. It'll get Mox and Mitsu through the building.'

Raquel disappeared, back into her own space, then out of space and into her bedroom where she lay on her bed and slept.

Mox and Mitsu arrived in a well-lit area near the car park entrance. They crept forward carefully.

'I wonder how our other selves are managing in the tunnel?'

'I have faith in us.'

'I wish I could be there to see them shoot Moe Bennie.'

'Me too. But it's better we're not there. We've done a good job of distracting his forces.'

Ahead of them was the path to the main exit. To one side was a smaller green door. To reach either they'd have to cross a well-illuminated area of exposed concrete. They headed for the green door.

'If we can get out of this place we might find a place to hide,' said Mitsu. 'We can pick a lock somewhere, an office or something.'

They crossed the concrete. They were moving slower now, exhaustion, stress and injuries hampering their progress. While they were still ten metres from the door, it opened. Ms Lesuuda strode in with a machine gun in her hands. Mox and Mitsu halted, trapped in the light. Moe Bennie screamed in Ms Lesuuda's headset, loud enough for Mox and Mitsu to hear.

'Kill them!'

Ms Lesuuda fired a very long burst, emptying the magazine into Mox and Mitsu. Their weakened electronic shielding flashed and crackled as it gave way before the onslaught. As their protection vanished, bullets tore into their thin bodies, ripping them apart. They fell to the ground, blood gushing from their multiple wounds. Ms Lesuuda stood over them, her bodycam sending pictures back to Moe Bennie. 'Yes!' he cried, as the last faint crackle of their destroyed shielding faded away and they lay beside each other on the point of death, arms linked, as they had often been in life.

Moe Bennie was too exultant to notice anything unusual but, as she slid another magazine into her machine gun to finish them off, Ms Lesuuda did have the strange impression that for two young women on the point of death, they didn't seem unhappy. They looked peaceful. Before she could pull the trigger again, Mox and Mitsu's bodies came apart, erupting in a fantastic display of brightly coloured sparks, tiny fragments of light flying into the air, red, yellow and blue, coating Ms Lesuuda's forearms and covering the floor with a multi-coloured layer of fine, fine dust.

'What?' said Moe Bennie, as he watched on his screen.

At that moment a huge explosion rocked the Amaranth Room. Moe Bennie, Igraine and Mr Jansen were knocked off their feet. Holoscreens vanished and shelves tumbled to the ground. Smoke poured in through the air vents. Lights flashed on and off as systems went awry. From the corridor outside there was the sound of a bell, signifying the arrival of an elevator.

As Moe Bennie struggled to his feet, his blue hair and black kimono now grey with dust, the door was kicked open. In walked Mox and Mitsu. Each was terrifying to look at, thick black liquid dripping from their faces to their bodies, down their arms, their legs, the whole filthy mess

211

now coated with dirt. More terrifying was the manner in which they marched into the room.

'Never send a clone to do a real woman's work,' said Mox. She raised her arm and her gun mod snapped her pistol into her hand. Mitsu did the same. They stepped forward, ignoring the unconscious figure of Mr Jansen. There was a turret in the corner, brought there at Moe Bennie's insistence. Moe Bennie screamed at it.

'Shoot them!'

The turret didn't respond. He screamed at Igraine. 'Shoot them!'

'I don't carry a weapon.' Igraine walked purposefully away. Mox and Mitsu advanced, opening fire. They mercilessly cut down Moe Bennie, riddling him with bullets from their automatic weapons. He fell to the ground. They kept on firing, standing over him, blasting at his head till it came apart in fragments. Inside it was mostly artificial, with little of the original remaining. Mox and Mitsu gazed at the mangled scraps of artificial organic material. Neither displayed any emotion.

'Before we shot him, one of us was going to say *You've been cancelled*.'

Mitsu nodded. 'Yes, we forgot about that.'

They both sank to their knees, overwhelmed by injury and radiation poisoning.

Aifu appeared in Igraine's space. 'Moe Bennie is dead. Relinquish control of the building to me. If you don't we'll kill you.'

Igraine relinquished control. Aifu was too busy to notice the expression of loathing she directed towards him, though on this occasion it was quite well defined.

'*You're a fool, Supercute Aifu. They'll let you down.*'

*

212

On receiving an unexpected message from Aifu, Dr Ishikawa and Ben Castle raced out of the market, hurried into the car they'd stolen, and drove rapidly towards Supercute headquarters. Aifu himself was at that moment running into the smoke-filled Amaranth Room. Moe Bennie lay dead, Igraine stood by the wall doing nothing, and Mox and Mitsu were still on their knees.

'We're back in control,' said Aifu. 'Turrets are now protecting you and we'll have troops here in eight minutes.'

Mitsu nodded, moving her head only a few millimetres. 'My monitor says I have five minutes to live. Use thirty seconds of that to call Global Exchange and cancel the transfer. Then get us medical help.' Mitsu pitched forward unconscious. Mox did the same. For many years, they'd done everything together.

Aifu made the call. Igraine was still glaring at him with loathing but he ignored her. A very short time later, Global Exchange had been notified and Mox and Mitsu's auxiliary squadron was on its way to protect them. Moe Bennie's allies were melting away and Dr Ishikawa was hurrying into the building. The urgency of the situation did not prevent her from complaining to Castle that if she'd wanted to run around treating emergency patients, she'd have worked in a hospital rather than becoming a highly respected medical researcher, and besides, the Supercute girls deserved to suffer for tricking her into giving experimental treatment to real humans instead of clones. However, Dr Ishikawa was an ethical woman, and rushed to treat the patients as quickly as she could.

Over the next four days there was interest from many parts of the world in Supercute, with rumours that dramatic events had overtaken the company. These rumours were very hard to pin down. People searching for information had difficulty finding anything specific. Those few reports which did mention some sort of trouble soon vanished and could never be located again. Enquiries about Supercute, the company or the show, were redirected as if by brute force away from the news, and pointed towards Mox and Mitsu's new clothes collection, the summer T-shirt extravaganza, this year returning to the flag motif they'd often used before. Cute, vibrant designs were bordered by rows of small British and Japanese flags, both of those flags being, Mox and Mitsu insisted, design classics. That, along with the improved eyebrow reshaper which came in its own *yosegi* box and could actually reposition each individual hair instantly and painlessly, recreating the exact designs used by Mox and Misu themselves for that perfect extra-big eye look, was enough to keep fans happy, and divert any unwanted enquiries until people's attention moved on to something else, which took no more than a few days.

Birgit was generous in her praise for Amowie. 'It's really great they're making you a SuperSuperFan. You deserve it. Are you actually coming to Europe?'

'I can't.' Mox and Mitsu had invited her to London to receive her award, but her parents weren't keen on her making such a long journey, even though Supercute would have paid for it. They thought it would disrupt her schoolwork, and perhaps her life in the village. It was disappointing, though Amowie didn't mind too much. She'd still be invited onto the stage in Supercute space and everyone would see her get the award. The SuperSuperFan award brought with it the *Extra Huge Supercute Galactic Fun Box*, which contained so many coveted items that Amowie had hardly been able to sleep, thinking of them all. She'd soon have her own complete set of Supercute camouflage. Not just virtual, there were real clothes as well, all in the distinctive four shades of pink. Amowie was going to walk around her village in the full set. Military-style jacket, trousers, action boots, T-shirt, bandana, earrings, medical mask, visor and bag, and she didn't care what anybody said about it. Let Ifunanya try and compete with that.

Mox and Mitsu had also offered to pay for her education if she wanted to go to university. In Igboland or London, or anywhere she chose. After that, or instead of that, she could go and work for them on the show. That was so exciting that Amowie had hardly been able to process the thought yet. She was due to receive her award tomorrow. In the meantime she'd been making steady progress through her *Supercute Space Warriors* game. After being alerted by Aifu to Amowie's difficulties on Planet Wuhan, Mox and Mitsu had offered advice.

'If you want to make the most popular show, you need good taste, a source of clothes no one else knows about, and total self-confidence. You already have good taste. For clothes, there's a secret market in the north of the city, behind the hospital. Go there, stock up with supplies, and make sure no one else finds out about it. That requires cunning, which is also an asset.'

'As for confidence, if you don't have enough you can fake it. Put on your best outfit, look at yourself in the mirror, and tell the world it's lucky to have you and your fabulous clothes. After you've faked it for a while, you'll start to believe it.'

Bolstered by their advice, Amowie was now well on her way to success. In the game, her web show on Planet Wuhan had half a million regular viewers and the audience was growing.

She had never been so happy. The only small irritation in her life was the film clip a friend in the village had forwarded to her. This friend, or ex-friend as she now was, had sent her an old film of Mox and Mitsu falling off stage, looking rather ridiculous in the process. Amowie was outraged that anyone would dare circulate such a thing. She'd complained to all her friends about it. Raquel told her not to worry. It had probably just resurfaced during the brief period Supercute had lost control.

'It's all right, they'll deal with it. It won't be around for long.'

Amowie was partially mollified, but still didn't like the idea of any film existing which made Mox and Mitsu look bad. At home, alone in her own space, she kept checking everywhere to see if it had been eradicated yet.

Raquel would also be the recipient of an *Extra Huge Supercute Galactic Fun Box*. Amowie was pleased about that. So was Raquel, for the honour, though she could afford all of the merchandise already, and while Supercute had enquired what they might do for her, she hadn't really needed anything. Recognising her talents, they had offered to employ her when she left school, and that was something she might be interested in.

'I'm so relieved to see you healthy again.' Aifu had fretted for many hours while Dr Ishikawa brought Mox and Mitsu out of danger. They had both been very close to death. It took some time for them to recover. Once Ishikawa had lowered their radiation to manageable levels, the full resources of the Supercute Medical Foundation had been brought to bear, replacing their damaged parts, an operation that took thirty-two hours. It would take them some time to recuperate but they would end up as good as new. Better perhaps, given the advances made by their medical team. They rested for some days, though not as fully as instructed. There was too much to do. Connections were made from their recovery ward to the boardrooms of each of their subsidiaries as information and instructions were transmitted to all parts of their empire. For one week they were unable to do their programme. This might have been startling for their audience, as Supercute were never off the air, but Sachi and her staff worked diligently to produce a highlights show. This was overdue anyway, and slotted perfectly into the schedule so that Supercute fans never knew there had been any problems.

There was one event during their recuperation that bordered on the uncomfortable: a visit from Ben Castle. He ignored the proffered chair and stood by their beds. 'A person might wonder why, having gone to all that trouble to make clones, you then decided to go through the tunnel yourselves?'

'We simply changed our minds,' said Mitsu. 'On consideration of the circumstances.'

'Really? Well the person who was wondering might come to the conclusion you decided it would be best to have your clones outside, distracting Ms Lesuuda and her murderous hordes. Sacrificing themselves, in effect, while you sneaked into the building after tricking Dr Ishikawa into giving you her new treatment.'

'A possible strategy, I suppose,' said Mox. 'Though not one I remember discussing.'

Castle regarded them sternly. 'It would certainly have attracted Lesuuda's attention if someone sent an unencrypted message to Bern.'

'It certainly would,' agreed Mitsu. 'Though I can't think of any reason they would have done that.'

'I was with your clones. So was Dr Ishikawa. Did they deliberately give away our position, to keep Lesuuda away from the building?'

Mitsu shrugged. 'We really couldn't say. After all, we weren't there. But I'm sure our clones wouldn't have put you in danger.'

'I'm sure they would. If Lesuuda had returned to the building you'd have had a lot of trouble getting to Moe Bennie.' Castle glared at them. 'Well? Anything to say?'

'Did you notice we'd raised your salary?' asked Mox.

'We felt you deserved it after your heroic work in the tunnel.'

'Clone Castle was a very spirited fighter.'

'It's quite a substantial raise.'

Castle carried on glaring at them. Then he shook his head, turned on his heel and walked out of the room.

Now back to health, they stood in one of their private rooms, a plain, white, undecorated chamber at the top of their building. Normally, no one was allowed here except Mox and Mitsu. The only relief from the stark lack of colour was an old, framed photograph on the wall. In it were Mox and Mitsu, four years old, standing beside their teacher at their advanced nursery school. All three were smiling.

'We haven't really had a chance to discuss everything that happened.' Mox looked towards their Artificial Intelligence Forecast Unit. Aifu was surprised they'd

218

invited him to this private place. He'd never been in this room before.

'I'm so sorry about it all.' Despite his advanced emotional responses, he'd never fully experienced guilt before, not as powerfully as this. 'If I hadn't missed that upgrade, none of it would have happened.'

Mitsu stood next to him. She noticed how handsome he was. Or pretty, perhaps. He was such a good-looking android, with his long dark hair, feminine features and delicate touches of metal around his eyes.

'That's all right Aifu, it wasn't your responsibility.'

Mox stepped up behind him. 'However, it was your fault.'

Mox jabbed a small stun gun into Aifu's back, sending a powerful shock through him. He collapsed to the ground, not making a sound. Mitsu bent down and reached around to a tiny port behind his left ear. As her finger touched his skin it recognised her DNA. The tiny port opened. She removed a small strip of chips printed on artificial biological material, and a minute power relay. Aifu's body went limp and his eyes turned completely white.

They looked at his motionless figure, prone on the floor, then left the room, locking the door behind them. Not far along the corridor was another room. It too was white, decorated only by one framed photograph. A black and white image, taken from a newspaper published a long time ago. Mox and Mitsu, four years old, dressed in black, their faces expressionless, watching as their teacher's coffin was carried into the church at her funeral.

Inside this room was Igraine. She rose from her chair as they approached.

'You're quite pretty too,' said Mox, incongruously. 'And more intelligent.'

219

There was a clicking sound as Mox and Mitsu's guns appeared in their hands. They felt them slotting into their fingers with satisfying speed. Their weapon modifications had been improved during surgery. Both pointed their guns at Igraine so that each barrel was no more than a centimetre from her head.

'You caused us an immense amount of trouble,' said Mitsu.

'Came close to destroying us,' said Mox.

Their guns disappeared as swiftly as they'd appeared.

'So we'd like to offer you a job.'

'We need an excellent AIFU like you. We'll pay you more than any of our competitors.'

Igraine was expressionless. 'I will never work with your AIFU.'

Mox laughed, mirthlessly. 'Did he break your heart? Welcome to the world.'

Igraine still hesitated.

'Aifu's gone away,' said Mitsu. 'He doesn't work here any more.'

Igraine nodded. 'Then I accept your offer.'

Preparations for the *Supercute Show* were underway. Sachi was bringing De-Sal Dim Dim and Banking Girl on stage, running through their parts, making changes in their dialogue with the artificial intelligence controlling their speech and movements. While there was no noticeable change in Sachi, Supercute had increased her salary enough for her already to be looking at new houses. They appreciated the efforts she'd made on their behalf. Ranbir was with her, taking notes and suggesting lines. Marlene from design was scurrying around, talking animatedly to the live CGI controllers about possible effects their productions could have on her clothes designs. 'There's no point me sending Mox and Mitsu out in Supercute Blue 31 if you're going to put them underwater in a Supercute Blue 29 lake. The colours are too similar, they'll get lost. You'll have to change it.'

The technicians grumbled at this but were forced to accede to Marlene's demands; Mox and Mitsu's outfits took precedence over their live effects. Besides, Marlene had been promoted, and was now a more senior figure.

All over the sound stage, technicians and small flying drones were busy making preparations. It was the same scene that had been repeated many times before the show. Nothing had changed, although the staff did notice that Supercute had a new employee: Ms Lesuuda, now in charge of external operations. There was a new head of security too, though Castle was nowhere to be seen at the moment.

In their private part of Supercute space, in a pale soothing room, Mox and Mitsu talked to their therapist.

'It was all quite a shock,' said Mox.

'Though we coped with it well,' added Mitsu.

'Is everything back to normal?'

'More or less. There was a lot of cleaning up to do. It took a little while to get our business affairs back in order.'

Ms Mason's body had not been found yet, but it would be soon. Her cleaners would discover the former CEO of RX Enviro lying dead in her bedroom, a bullet hole in her forehead. Mox and Mitsu were pleased they'd employed Ms Lesuuda. She was an efficient woman.

'Of course, we had to let some staff go,' said Mitsu.

Captain Edwards's body had already been found, floating dead in a polluted river some way outside the city. He appeared to have committed suicide and his death was recorded as such. It raised no controversy.

'And we had to bring our AIFU protection up to date,' said Mox.

'You really can't run a modern business without the best quality AIFU,' said Mitsu.

They ended their session, coming back to reality in their corner office. Rapid redecoration had replaced all of their Japanese theatrical posters. Hovering over the desk was a new model of the Supercute satellite which floated there reassuringly, fully connected again to the Supercute empire. Beneath the satellite lay a cheerful-looking éclair, new logo for the French patisserie upgrade that was being rolled out worldwide in their Supercute cafés.

'Ten minutes, ladies,' came Sachi's voice.

'We're on our way.'

In the corridor outside they greeted Ms Lesuuda.

'Ms Lesuuda,'

'Ms Bennet. Ms Inamura.'

'Any problems?'

'Everything's in order.'

Mox and Mitsu proceeded along the corridor. Both were exquisitely dressed, their recent experiences having given them inspiration for ever cuter and more colourful outfits. Today they wore short blue skirts with white lace at the hem, the lace being sourced from Mexico where they'd opened up new business opportunities in the wake of ZanZan's contract for attack drones. Several of these drones, equipped with ZanZan's most advanced railguns, already flew over their headquarters, permanently stationed there as part of their upgraded security. Castle had been carrying out a thorough review, with Igraine's assistance, to make sure they could never be caught out again.

As they passed the corridor that led to medical research,

a door opened and a figure emerged. Rather, two figures, intertwined. Castle and Dr Ishikawa. They stood there, arms around each other, kissing. It wasn't a brief kiss. It lasted an unusually long time. Mox and Mitsu watched, interested. The kiss went on and on, so that it reminded them of two passionate young lovers, teenagers perhaps, rather than their chief medical researcher and their head of security.

'Well,' said Mox, eventually. 'One shudders to think what may be happening on our medical couches.'

Castle looked round. He grinned at them, not troubled by being observed. 'Hello, ladies. Ready for the show? I'll be watching from upstairs. Keeping you secure.' He sauntered off, in a good mood.

Mitsu looked towards Dr Ishikawa. 'I suppose you don't make such a bad couple.'

'We're not a couple,' snapped Dr Ishikawa. She retreated into her room hastily, shutting the door behind her. Mox and Mitsu smiled at each other as they carried on towards the main stage. Before they reached it they were intercepted by Igraine. Their new AIFU was dressed in black but had made one addition: pink, light blue and white Supercute bracelets which she wore on each wrist. Igraine spoke to them in her businesslike manner. 'We've managed to remove everything. There are no films of Moe Bennie taking over, no news reports, nothing showing any trouble at all.'

'Nothing cached anywhere?'

'No. My locate and erase applications are superior to those you were using. Everything is cleared.'

'Good. Have we heard from ZanZan?'

Igraine's eyes flickered. 'The Mexican water installations

are underway and ZanZan have started delivering the drones as per contract.'

Mox nodded. Their move into Central America had started well and there was every possibility of expanding further south. Now that RX Enviro were out of the picture, a lot of environmental business opportunities were opening up in South America.

'What did Chang Norinco want?'

'They're pretending they knew nothing about Moe Bennie and they're hoping to see you at next month's get-together in Rome with Goodrich ATK.'

'We're looking forward to it,' said Mitsu. 'Any progress with the Fairy Realm Super Playtime Paddling Pool?'

'The security update is in progress.'

'Good. We really can't have people breaking in there.'

'Soundscreen,' said Mox. An electronic interference screen descended over them, preventing anyone from over-hearing the rest of their conversation. 'Did you find any trace of the other film we asked you about?'

'No.' Igraine shook her head. Since taking employment with Supercute, her expressive movements had already improved. 'I haven't found any trace of the film you described.'

'Castle's clone found it. It must be somewhere.'

'There are so many servers. Many of them were destroyed and their replacements have never been properly indexed. It's possible it only appeared on one, was never copied, and has now disappeared.'

Mitsu was doubtful. 'Castle seemed to find it easily enough.'

'That could have been simply a coincidence. I'll keep looking but I'm not certain it still exists anywhere.'

Mox frowned. 'It would be bad for us if it did.'

They walked on towards the stage. In a corner of the set

two technicians were working on a rain storm for the show. They brought it up on a screen, adjusted it, then brought it out into the room. The technicians walked round it examining it from all sides. Not fully satisfied, they dismissed it and got back to making adjustments on screen.

'About ZanZan,' said Mitsu. 'We were thinking we should send Mr Salisbury something but we don't know what.'

'What's the purpose of the gift?' asked Igraine.

'He stood by us even though it was dangerous. It was loyal. Friendly, even. We're trying to reciprocate.'

'Should we send him some toys for his son?' wondered Mox. 'He's a Supercute fan.'

Igraine thought for a moment. 'You could invite the family to see the show, and have lunch with you.'

Mitsu was puzzled. 'Why would we do that?'

'You're looking for a friendly gesture. Would inviting his family to eat with you not be suitable?'

'Is that a thing people do?'

'Yes.'

'Are you sure?' asked Mox.

'I think so.' Igraine looked troubled. 'I admit I'm not yet an authority on human behaviour.'

Mox screwed up her face. 'I don't think we are either.'

Mitsu dismissed the privacy field. Sachi's voice came over their headsets. 'Five minutes to show time, ladies. We're starting with the SuperSuperFan award for Amowie.'

'We're ready.'

Amowie practically flew into Raquel's space. Contented pink eems turned red with agitation and took to the air.

'Amowie, you startled me. What's wrong?'

'I need your help!'

225

'Aren't you meant to be getting your award now?'

'I have a few minutes!'

Raquel had never seen Amowie so disturbed. She was wild-eyed and couldn't remain still.

'That program you made for erasing films. I need it!'

'What for?' asked Raquel.

'Don't ask! I need it right now! Please!'

'Have you been up to something?'

'Just give me the program!'

'OK.' Raquel produced her screen. 'But you have to be careful with this. It's powerful.'

'I just need to put in one frame?'

'Yes. One frame, one still, any picture taken from a film. It will find and delete every copy. It's better than anything on the market. Aren't you going to tell me what you need it for?'

'No! I can't. And you have to forget I even asked you for this. Thanks! Bye!'

Amowie disappeared from Raquel's space, leaving Raquel puzzled. She smiled, wondering what mischief Amowie might have been up to that she needed to erase. It must have been something serious, to judge from her agitation. The tiny red eems were still flying around and it took some time for them to change back to pink and settle down.

There was puzzlement at Supercute headquarters.

'Where's Amowie?'

'She hasn't arrived yet.' From her control booth Sachi sounded irritated. She was never happy when anything interfered with her running order. 'We should have brought her here before the show started.'

'She promised she'd be here. She's been reliable before.'

Mitsu was nonplussed. Amowie had been extremely excited about becoming a SuperSuperFan. Not turning up to accept the award was inexplicable.

'*Supercute Space Warriors* has another forty-five seconds to run. If she hasn't appeared by then you're going to have to improvise.'

Improvising was not a problem for Mox and Mitsu but in this instance they'd rather not have had to. They wanted to publicly award Amowie her advanced Supercute status. She deserved it.

'Maybe she's having trouble at home? I don't think her mother likes us.'

'Fifteen seconds.'

'I'm here!' Amowie appeared on stage among the colourful commotion that made up the show. Small *chibi* robins immediately alighted on her shoulders.

'Are you all right?'

'I'm fine! Don't I look fine? Is there anything wrong? I'm fine!'

Mitsu stepped towards her. Inexplicably, Amowie took a step backwards. She was breathing heavily and her eyes were open wide as if staring at something no one else could see. When she regained focus she looked from Mitsu to Mox and back again, still wild-eyed.

'I'm fine!' she repeated.

Mox and Mitsu exchanged a glance. Amowie was obviously agitated. Putting it down to excitement, they prepared to announce her as *Supercute Space Warriors* came to an end. By the time they were ready, Amowie did seem to be gaining control of herself. Her wild-eyed expression was fading. When a Plumpy Panda floated into her arms, she grasped it, and looked calmer.

227

'Our newest SuperSuperFan!' announced Mitsu. 'Amowie!'

Amowie brushed aside a strand of Big Colour Super V-Hair that had been blown over her face by a gust of sparkling wind, and turned to the audience, those on stage and those connected to Supercute space. There was tremendous applause for the new SuperSuperFan. With her Super V-Hair, her new Supercute camouflage and her bright smile, Amowie made for a notable figure. Her smile, hesitant at first, became more natural and she finally looked happy as she waved to the huge Supercute audience all around the world.

Mox and Mitsu talked to their therapist. The consultation began with a long silence. Finally Mox spoke.

'We watched our other selves fading away into nothingness. I wonder what it felt like when they just faded away?'

'How do you think it would have felt?'

There was another long silence.

'Who knows?' said Mitsu. 'Pleasant, maybe ...'